BLUE RASPBERRY

REMO NASSUTTI

For Brittan

Outcast Press

Fiction From the Fringes

Cover by Cody Sexton of AThinSliceOfAnxiety.com

Formatted and edited by Paige Johnson, author of *Percocet Summer* and *Citrus Springs*

www.Outcast-Press.com

(e-book) ASIN: B0FJYX39VJ

(print) ISBN-13: 978-1-960882-18-9

"Blue Raspberry *reads like a transmission from the edge of adolescence and America. It's a new classic for the medicated, alienated, over-stimulated generation.*"

—Neda Aria, author of *Red Wings* and *Us, Women*

"*A sorrowful dirge to a lost generation raised on anti-depressant cocktails,* Blue Raspberry *is powerful and poignant, beautiful and existentially disturbing, passing like summer under a diseased sky.*"

—Coy Hall, author of *The Owl Men of Shanidar*

"With shades of Kids, Saltburn, *and* The Graduate, Blue Raspberry *is a coming-of-age West Coast homage to the post-Y2K era. A sharply written debut novel about lost boys, lost innocence, and the millennial young adult experience."*

—Wendy Dalrymple,
author of *Credenza* and *Birthday Party Demon*

"I don't like painting flowers in my music. I like painting guts and pain."

—Jonathan Davis,
singer of Korn

I DREAMED MY FEET WERE FULL OF BEES

I want you to do something for me. Picture a young man. He will never be the shortest or the tallest person in the room. Built like a runner, he keeps his hair like a surfer would. He wears his T-shirts and sweatshirts until the seams split and grow dark with dirt. As far as colors, he prefers blue, black, and olive drab.

The young man I'm talking about, Calvin, sits before a piano. He lifts the key cover and slides it back and away to play. He warms up his hands with the D minor scale. I know he loves this particular key, that he loves the sorrow in the notes.

Let me tell you a little about the room. The walnut wood piano sits in a corner in front of a bookshelf. Upon the shelf, march novels and family photos and carved bookends. Above the piano hangs a light fixture; below the piano stretches a rose-gold carpet.

Across the room, upon a couch, I make a space for myself. My body warms a spot on the cold leather, which makes it difficult to leave.

At the piano, Calvin compresses a handful of keys that, together, make a lonesome sound. One can imagine the hills that stand like a great wall between this house and the Pacific Ocean.

Calvin plays a chord, and I can feel the sound of it in the back of my neck—a chord like a stretched rubber band.

"E diminished," he says. "Some people hate the diminished chord. I think it sounds like anticipation. It wants to go home. You never want to end a song on this chord."

Then he plays the chord he started with.

"D minor," he says. "Some call it the saddest key, but maybe, in its sorrow, we find a bit of relief."

A few hours later, we take a walk towards the peak of some nearby hill. The day shines—a moment between rainy seasons. The first days of the schoolyear loom. So, we look to the hills and climb. The sun sinks, falling in a slow dive toward the horizon. We pass patches of trees and wander away from trails, dead summer grass waving in the breeze. Evening takes a slow turn towards night.

When we reach the top of the hill, we take in a view of our neighborhood. We see a thousand dollhouses. Lights glitter like rhinestones. Streets and roadways enforce a strict grid. Up north, we can see the Dumbarton Bridge lay across San Francisco Bay like a beaded necklace. The bridge links together bedazzled clusters of honeycomb houses. In each of those dollhouses, a problem waits for us. But from here, they seem so small and pointless.

We stand, studying the scenery for as long as it takes to catch our breath, and then we speak.

Calvin looks at me and says, "I dreamed my feet were full of bees."

If it were up to me, this is the moment the story would have ended. I'd have said, "That's it." Then a fade to black, a popular song cutting in over the credits. There's only so long I can call things glittering or bedazzled. Nobody wants to hear about the trees and the grasses. No one cares for the long winding lines of traffic.

But since you want to keep reading, I'll tell you the rest of the story. Though you should know that it'll be a waste of your time. You could be doing anything else. You'd enjoy yourself a lot better.

But anyway.

RAINFALL

We don't see it coming, but I guess we never do. The black SUV barrels down the street and hits a backed-up gutter. A fan of grimy water arcs towards Calvin and me. Our sweaters suck the cold up. A smell like leaf rot and motor oil and decomposing fast-food wrappers. Then the one-two punch. One of the big tires stomps into a pothole and launches one last salvo.

The luxury vehicle continues down the road and around the corner.

"Fuck!"

"Shoulda taken the bus." Calvin wrings out his sweater.

For days, unseasonal rainwater has filled up many potholes along the road. The gutters don't drain right, so they filled up, too.

We stand at a corner. Down the street, extends a row of multi-story houses. On a fence post, a cat stands, wet fur matted.

"Bravest cat in the world," Calvin says.

We walk past a fairground. Except it isn't a fairground because summer is ending. When it isn't July, it's just a field. And when it isn't July, it's muddy and clumped like the cat's fur.

The fairground sits between mansions. These homes cost as much as a whole town in one of those flyover states. Except, if we're being honest, some of these homes cost as much as a whole flyover state.

"Think of all that money." I shake my head. "You'd think they could fix the roads."

"I'm freezing," Calvin says.

The stretch of houses ends at the mouth of the main drag. Shops and chain stores link together from end to end.

We enter a hardware store. It sits next door to the pharmacy I use. You can spot it by the big glowing doctor's caduceus—you know the two snakes wrapped up together. Anyway, inside the neighboring hardware store, we search out the ceramic heater aisle and turn the largest floor model to the max.

Hands cupped around the heater's hot grill, Calvin asks, "You wanna hear a ghost story?"

A lady passes through the aisle and keeps her eyes on us like watching a snake.

"Sure."

"Last year," he says, "this kid laid down on the tracks and let the Northbound 12:15 take him away."

"Which one was that?" I ask. "There were a couple last year."

He shrugs, "The train hammered his class ring flat. His sister kept it. She used to walk down to the tracks with the ring in her pocket. On some nights, she saw what looked like her brother walking along the tracks."

"Coulda been anyone."

"No." He pushes his hands right up to the mouth of the heater. "When you see something like that, you can't get too near it. Shoots this ice-cold water all through you. She could feel that it was a ghost."

"Weird."

"At first, she didn't mind seeing him. But, after a while, she started to think that he couldn't move on. So, she flattened the ring until it could fit in the coin slot on the train. She slid it in and rode to San Francisco for the day. Never saw him again."

"Bullshit."

"Nah." He shakes his head.

My birthday lands on the first Thursday of the schoolyear. I run to the fence in my backyard and turn at an angle to see Calvin's window. I wave and, a few minutes later he arrives at my front door.

"How'd you know I'd be at my desk?" he asks.

"Lucky guess. Plus, could see your silhouette."

We smoke a blunt behind a Safeway in the Heights then walk past our old grade school.

"I had therapists," he says. "They felt like Hollywood remakes. They each found different ways of making me tell the same stupid stories."

I wish I could respond with a few words like an actor does. Add a big dramatic pause and leave the audience feeling satisfied.

Instead, I nod and shrug.

We meet with Greg outside of a local diner. The burger place is a death trap for anyone with a peanut allergy. You'll find shells littering the floor like shredded newspaper at the bottom of a birdcage.

College students drink late summer beers out front.

"Guess you'll get your license now," Greg says, slapping me on the arm.

We slide around the building and perch by the dumpsters. Greg kills the roach.

"Where's Jacqueline?" I ask.

"Probably fighting her mom," he says.

Greg coughs from the blunt and rubs his chest. The sort of thin chest that fathers despise. "My sister keeps calling my house," Greg says. "She just graduated from Cal Poly. Has these big wheezy anxiety attacks over the phone with my dad."

"Weird," Calvin says.

"Yeah, my dad's been a fucking dick to me about my grades. Says that this year will be my last chance." Greg slips his phone from his pocket and dials Jacqueline. "No answer. We'll crash her place. Give me a minute."

He burns his fingers trying to light the roach one last time.

Jacqueline runs down her driveway and meets us on the sidewalk. The tie-dyed lavender and violet skies droop over us—thin clouds stretched to wisps. She kisses Greg, mashing their lips together.

We travel to a nearby park with a slowness like summer will never end. We all make the kind of promises to each other that go like, "This year will be different," or "I'll never, never, never, *not ever* be like my parents."

The park provides an oasis inside an oasis. University Heights swims in seas of iceplants—we used to break their green stalks open to pen our names on park benches. They crawl up hillsides where sprawling houses perch, purple flowers opening each year just in time for Valentine's Day. The whole area gives you the sense that someone tried to build a siege-proof castle. Somewhere to stow the plunders of the silicon age.

An afternoon train roars in the distance. The line dumps passengers at stops all along the peninsula.

"I could be eating plastic for all I know," Jacqueline says. She speaks in a husky, loud voice, as though you might forget her if she doesn't keep up the volume.

Greg laughs. "Okay, babe."

"No, for real." Jacqueline slaps her hands together. "Have you ever smelled your medications in the morning?"

"Oh," I say, "the taste, too."

"He gets it. Just like plastic. A sorta fake taste."

"Yeah, it's nasty." Greg makes a face.

"Could be plastic." Jacqueline shrugs.

"What would the point of feeding us plastic be?" Greg asks.

"Okay," Jacqueline says in a mock conspiratorial tone. "So, we can't get rid of plastic, it lasts forever, hard to break down. What if, like, we ground plastic up and put it in pills. That way we could run it through the digestive tracts of every kid in America. Recycling."

Calvin rolls his eyes.

"Easy to market. Tell parents it'll make their kids behave. Next, it's in every home."

"You're crazy," I say.

"You're all too fucking serious. But the stuff really does smell and taste like plastic, so I had to make up a reason for it. I don't mind my meds. They're a nice legal high that makes life more tolerable."

I meet Calvin on the way to the bus stop. The cold blue morning hangs over us.

Calvin wraps his sweater tight. "The last time a kid died on the tracks, people all said they saw or heard it. But what they saw or heard was all different. Someone said they heard him cry out like a lost child. Some say he gave an eloquent speech about how he never had an unscheduled minute in his entire life. Some say he threw the world's biggest tantrum."

I go to shrug.

After a beat, I say, "I think I get it."

He nods.

"We've all heard the same story before," I say. "We all know someone who took the train. So, all those people filled in their own details."

He crosses his arms.

He says, "All winds up together, like a mosaic."

SEVENTH GRADE DRUGS

Korn releases a new single, and the rain breaks. A good day to take the bus halfway home and walk the rest.

"I can't believe you take Celexa," Jacqueline says to me. "So seventh grade of you."

"She's right," Greg says.

The two of them walk along the sidewalk. Jacqueline wears an olive-green polo with an embroidered bird logo. Greg's skinny, pale arms stick out the bottom of his baggy sleeves.

I try to stay abreast, scraping into the occasional bush. "Why?"

"It's the first one any doctor will start you on," Jacqueline says.

"Well," Greg says, "not always. It depends. The doctor might have a deal with another drug company."

"True," she says.

"Then what do you take?" I ask. "Because you must be so much cooler than me."

"My mom said I was so fucked up that I needed the serious stuff," she says. "Doctor started me on Seroquel. But I may need to get some stronger stuff."

Greg cuts in. "You know when people call an old car a classic?"

"Yeah?"

"I take Prozac, the classic car of anti-depressants." He grins. Then reaches out to drape his arm over Jacqueline's shoulder, tugging her close. They sway side-to-side along the sidewalk.

Seeing this, I pull my shoulders together, push my chest out, flex my arms.

Jacqueline lifts her right arm and takes Greg's dangling hand. Their fingers interlace. Cracks and chips show in her red nail polish. Cars swoosh past us, sucking on air.

We turn onto a little side street of double-decker houses.

"Here we are," Jacqueline says. She waves to a house. An old gold Lexus sedan sits, sunbathing in the driveway, unwashed and dusty.

We walk past it, and Jacqueline kicks a tire with her toe.

"This will be mine when I get my license."

"Oh, cool," I say.

"Though my dad should buy me something for my sweet sixteen next month." She draws a line through the dust with a finger.

Greg looks like a second backpack, swinging from one arm.

Jacqueline says, "My dad has a Lambo, so it's the least he can do."

"For real?" I ask.

"Yeah, he moved to Portugal or Malta or something. He could get me a BMW or a Benz." She wipes the dust off on her jeans.

"My parents already said they won't get me shit," Greg says.

"That sucks," I say.

Jacqueline releases Greg's hand, and he opens and closes his fingers a few times. She climbs a set of short steps to her front door. Greg and I stand at the bottom of the stoop as Jacqueline digs in her backpack for her keys. A cluttered lanyard clangs and rattles out of the backpack. Bits of the brass finish on the door handle flaked off long ago. She jams the key in the lock and twists it open.

Inside, a white, fluffy, yapping dog charges us. Its nails skitter across the floor. Its tongue hangs out of its mouth, small and red.

Jacqueline bends down and coos at the dog, "These are friends."

Clutter overtakes the kitchen. Stinking dishes soak in the sink. A saucepan—caked with marinara—sticks to the granite countertop. Another saucepan tops the stove, full of cloudy water.

"*Aghh*," Jacqueline says, sliding the pan off the stove. The pan screeches across the burner. The sound makes me bite the inside of my cheek. "My brother left this shit out," she says and dumps the gray water onto the dishes in the sink.

She slams the pot down.

"Either of you want ramen?" she asks.

"Nah," Greg says.

"I'm good."

"In a bit then. Fuck, it'd be great if my mom wasn't so lazy. Hire a cleaner. Everyone else does."

She stands in the kitchen, staring at the saucepan in her hand. As she looks up, the motion causes her long, blonde hair to swing back and forth over the tops of her shoulders. She stands there, flexing her fingers on the pan until I say, "I'm fine chilling."

"Yeah," Greg says.

"Okay, we can go upstairs."

She leads us up her staircase to an empty, dark hall. We follow into her pale blue room.

Bits of photographs decorate the walls, held on by Scotch tape. Some of the photos show Jacqueline and her friends. Some are clippings from magazines. Images Hillary Duff in *Lucky* and Avril Lavigne from *Cosmopolitan*: Jacqueline's own little style board. A poster hangs on tacks, one corner torn. It reads *March of the Penguins*.

A bunched-up comforter lays at the foot of her bed, half of it hanging off.

Jacqueline swings her backpack by one strap. The contents *thump* hard as the bag hits the floor. Greg tosses his backpack down, too. The zippers make sharp sounds against the bare wood. The two of them slide into the bed together.

Checking the spots to sit, I head to the rug and take off my backpack.

Jacqueline pulls the crumpled comforter up over herself and Greg. She almost knocks a brass lamp off her nightstand in the process. Greg returns his arm to her shoulder.

I remove my shoes and line them up next to my backpack.

Jacqueline digs in her nightstand and pulls out an orange pill bottle. She tosses it to me. "Check those out," she says. "Seroquel. You want one right now?"

"Can I have one, too?" Greg asks.

"Sure, babe."

The bottle contains round, salmon-colored pills.

"Shit or get off the pot," she says to me.

"Sure." I take one out.

"There're some beers in the mini-fridge next to you."

I put the pill in my mouth. It starts to dissolve on my tongue: an awful, bitter taste. Jacqueline takes the bottle back.

Inside the fridge sit a couple cans of Bud Light.

"My mom never checks in there," Jacqueline says, taking a pill. "Give me a beer." She passes the pill bottle to Greg, and I hand her a beer. Then I open one for myself.

The Bud Light takes the pill down easy.

"This shit cleans you the fuck out," Jacqueline says. "Lets you sleep. You feel like someone pulled all those stupid fucking thoughts out of your head."

"Sounds wonderful," Greg says.

"Why didn't I ever hear about this?"

"Keep up with the times."

We listen to the new Korn song, "Twisted Transistor," and then the Seroquel starts to hit.

My tongue feels like a sponge in the hot sun. The train of thought runs off the rails, and I lean against the wall.

Greg wraps himself up close to Jacqueline and kisses her ear. She throws her head back.

"I told you this shit is nice," she says. "Not a high or anything, but, fuck, is it nice to calm the fuck down for a minute."

I close my eyes. Through my eyelids, the sun from the window lights my world in the orange-red of my own blood. When I rub my eyes, the orange-red turns to a honeycomb pattern of gold and black. All that seems to exist is me rubbing my eyes, on the carpet, in this room.

A while later, I go to the bathroom. On the wall, hang two framed photographs. One shows a handful of thick and pointed seashells laying on sand. In the other picture, a night-shot of a Ferris wheel, strings of lights sparkling along the spokes.

A potpourri of branches tops the toilet bowl. I wash my hands with cold water and cool my hot face with damp hands.

Back in the room.

Greg and Jacqueline lie across the bed. Eyes flutter, half-closed, drifting back and forth across the ceiling. Arms sprawl, palms open. Then they get very still and close their eyes. For a moment, looking at their bodies, draped and motionless, and looking at the way they sink into the mattress, it's almost like...

Hear the wailing that starts in the distance and screams towards us. The navy-blue uniforms and sky-blue nitrile gloves shuffle into the house. They take my friends and cover them up because gazing upon them too long is like staring into the sun. When the white sheets float out of the building like ghosts on Halloween, you feel their absence. Even if you don't see them exit, you feel it. Then they scoop me up. Someone squeezes me and tells me, "It's going to be okay," which might be the sweetest thing you can say to someone. Sweeter than "I love you."

They take me and erase my homework assignments and middle-of-the-road grades. When I walk through school, everyone has the eyes of a forgiving god. Then they say that Celexa was such a seventh-grade drug. So, they give me the salmon-colored Seroquel tablets that wash my mind clean.

...and then Jacqueline sighs and shifts and Greg scratches his ass. The sun reflects off the white comforter. I shield my eyes from the light because gazing upon them too long is like staring into the sun.

I sit back down at the foot of the bed on the little carpet.

CANDY

Bags of candy corn pile high, heaping against the inside of the drugstore windows. They look like lost teeth. They look like a schoolyear in motion.

Jacqueline leans against the window. Behind her, five-pound fun-size variety packs. Behind her, cardboard witches on broomsticks, black cats.

Speaking of candy, we all have candy-colored pills lined up with our breakfasts. The coating tastes sweet and sticks to our tongues.

And a kid shoves out of the store. A flash of music from the days of the Berlin Wall escapes: Annie Lennox singing about the rain coming back. The kid pulls a bag of candy from the sleeve of a tan jacket. He holds it up like a trophy.

The doors squeeze shut. The music becomes synthetic drums inside of a glass jar.

Speaking of jars. Keep your bottles of candy-colored pills in a row, labels facing forward. Buy one of those Sunday-through-Saturday containers like you live in an old folk's home. Swallow these pills to control your impulses.

Speaking of control, let's talk about my friend, Kevin. His parents watch him take his lithium tablets each morning. He says he sticks his tongue out Michael Jordan-style for them. They feed him tablets because he used to open up the capsules—one at a time—and dump out the powder inside. They found him out because he stopped making a fuss about taking the pills—something was up.

Speaking of Kevin...

"Where the fuck is Greg?" Jacquline says.

Sunlight reaches over the buildings on the opposite side of the street. The beams of light drag red undertones from her blonde hair.

Behind me, my buddy Reiner hovers. "What ya doing, man?" he says, sneaking up, breath tickling my ear.

I swat at him like he's a bug.

Jacqueline laughs, then coughs. "You're so stupid."

Calvin stands apart from us. His hair drapes over his eyes. Behind him, costume props hang on hooks. Pre-packaged costumes that smell like something I can't quite find the name for. They smell like our candy-colored pills.

He looks at the costumes and says, "Do you guys say, 'butcher knife' or 'butcher's knife'?"

Jacqueline pulls her phone out and dials something. She puts it to her ear.

"Wake me up when September ends," Reiner says.

Jacqueline covers the receiver with one hand and says, "It did end, dipshit."

"It's a song, dipshit," Reiner says.

Down the street, we see Greg appear.

Jacqueline snaps her phone shut.

Greg greets us and kisses Jacqueline.

"Let's say hi to Kevin," Jacqueline says. "I got something important to ask him."

She opens the door, and we head inside.

Kids pile their backpacks at the end of the candy aisle. You might spot the kids down the aisle, checking out the colorful packages.

A tall teenager in a red vest pushes a wide mop across the speckled tile floor, erasing muddy footprints.

"Hey, Kevin," Jacqueline says to the guy in the red vest.

He turns, tongue flicking at the stainless-steel knobs that pierce his lips. He asks us to follow him down the personal care aisle. More muddy tracks. The kids go to gawk at lube and condoms.

Kevin says, "Did you hear about the dude who took all his pills last weekend?" He leans on his broom like discussing sports.

"Yeah," Jacqueline says. "Used to drive by his house. California ranch style. Always two cars in the driveway. Mercedes and BMW."

"His dad kept servers in the garage," Kevin says, nodding. "I'd take the train if it were me."

"Why?" Calvin asks.

"Because you stop traffic for an hour or two." Kevin resumes his mopping.

Greg says he has to pee. That he'd been at the recording studio at the rec center. That he has a CD for Kevin when he gets back. Real punk shit.

Reiner follows Greg to piss.

"I want to buy some candy," Jacqueline says to Kevin.

"Then buy some," Kevin says. He notices that we brought mud in, too. So, he goes to cover our tracks.

"No," Jacqueline says. "Like *candy* candy."

"Okay," Kevin says. "So, like?"

"I need to chill out," Jacqueline says. "Wish I had pills they give to people who fear flying."

"We all need to chill out," Kevin says. "They said the kid had IED, like his older brother. That's 'something explosive' disorder."

"Intermittent," Jacqueline tries to wedge into his rant.

"You know anyone who needs to chill out? You know what I mean?"

"Like the bombs overseas. They call those IEDs, too," Kevin says. "But instead, it's kids here." Kevin's mop squeaks across the floor. We turn down the medicine aisle. Rows and rows of colorful boxes of pills. "I think Sarah hates flying," Kevin says. "Her and Charlotte. Two big babies about planes."

"Sarah's so cute," Jacqueline says. She looks at Calvin and me.

Speaking of cuteness. The candy-colored pills slash the Latin drug names. Instead, we get something that sounds like onomatopoeia. Bupropion, Celexa, Prozac, Klonopin. In the medicine aisle, a thousand other such names.

Jacqueline says, "Haven't seen Sarah since that pool party this summer."

Kevin nods. "I see her every day in class."

"Good to know she's afraid of flying," Jacqueline says. "Put a word in about that."

Kevin nods. "Except, you know, it's California. We're prone to droughts."

"Yeah, I get it," she says.

At the end of the aisle, several walkers lie on the ground.

"Fucking kids." Kevin picks them up.

Greg and Reiner return from the toilet.

"My turn," Jacqueline says and hands her backpack to Greg. She disappears.

"I want candy," Greg says.

Kevin rolls his eyes. "What kind?"

"Chocolate," Greg says. "Let's go get some."

Kevin leans the mop against an end cap. We walk to the candy aisle. The mountain of backpacks has grown since we last saw it. Kevin boots the pile with one of his Doc Martens, sending dusty packs across the floor.

The kids in the aisle all look but don't say shit.

"By the way," Greg says, "I also want drugs."

"Of course," Kevin says.

Greg taps his nose with one index finger.

"Okay, noted," Kevin says and nods.

Greg grabs a bag of chocolates off the shelf. He puts one finger up in front of his lips and stuffs the bag into his interior jacket pocket.

"Sir," Kevin says in a loud voice.

Greg hisses past that single finger.

"With three layers of nougat, you're making a wise investment," Kevin says.

"Shut up."

Jacqueline returns, and we say our goodbyes.

The sun is hiding when we get outside. We cross the street and wait at the bus stop.

Greg pulls the bag of candy from his jacket. He grins like a vampire bat. "Anyone want some?"

Calvin stares across the street at the storefront. Someone has switched on black-and-orange string lights in the window display.

Greg rips the package open, dropping several candies to the ground.

Jacqueline asks Calvin, "What are you thinking about?"

"That I've been saying 'butcher knife' for years, but that it's probably more correct to say, 'butcher's knife.'" He shrugs.

"It's definitely, 'butcher knife,'" Greg says. He unwraps a candy and hands one to Reiner.

Calvin says, "Then I start thinking that butchery is a fast way to go, but childhood dies the slowest death."

Greg and Reiner laugh.

"You all are so stupid," Jacqueline says.

Without the sun reaching over the buildings, her blonde hair looks gray.

CREATINE

"Here," my father said, "drink this."

This was around the turn of the millennium or something like that.

He offered me a glass of cloudy water that—when I drank it—tasted like licking wet cement. My father drank the same thing.

He said, "What are you? A lightweight?"

"More like a flyweight," I said.

"Then that drink will help," he said, leaning on the kitchen counter. "Drink it every morning."

That was the year after the divorce.

"Here, drink this."

"Are you a heavyweight yet?"

"No, still a flyweight."

My father bought a tub of white powder and kept it by the liquor cabinet. Colorful pictures wrapped around the tub, displaying powerful biceps.

One tablespoon per glass of water. Stir. Drink with your morning coffee.

My father noticed the strange way I walked down the hallway. How I stepped on specific boards. He worked in market research or something. This was the time for science.

He put a rubber band around my wrist. Told me to use it whenever I felt the need to step on those specific spots. "Pull back that band and let it snap against the inside of your wrist. A corrective measure. You gotta build a negative association."

My wrists blistered.

"Here, drink this."

"Are you a heavyweight yet?"

"Bantamweight."

He asked me if I still avoided glue.

I shrugged.

Using glue means washing your hands raw. Wash. Because the idea of gluing your urethra shut when you go to pee—and your bladder filling then bursting—is too much to bear. It also means rubbing the end of the penis raw with a washcloth for good measure.

On the plus side, using the bathroom means an extra opportunity to check out your muscles in the mirror. Maybe the powder drink was working.

"Are you a heavyweight yet?"

"Featherweight."

The blisters became callouses.

My father said, "Squat! Bench Press! Curl! Pull!"

My father said enough of that would take away the fears.

Focus. Blood engorges exerted muscles. Feel the pump. Hear the pounding music and the clattering of iron plates. While you're at it, look at that cute girl who rides the stationary bike. Maybe you could date her and that would make those behaviors stop.

My father said only whining narcissists go to therapists. Only the very emotional. Only the weak. And if—one day you could bench press a mid-sized sedan—then you'd never need therapy. Because only the new generation or neurotic women or hysterical women or your mother went to therapists.

My father said that medicine meant you suffered the same weakness.

My father said, "Here, drink this."

"Are you a heavyweight yet?"

"Lightweight."

The callouses split open.

My father said that doctors weren't therapists. Doctors dealt with real problems. So, a psychiatrist—who's a real doctor—could help. For once, he and my mother agreed on something.

This doctor worked from a dusty office. This doctor pointed patients towards sofas instead of examining tables. She kept a shelf of books instead of blood pressure cuffs and stethoscopes.

She said, "Obsessive-compulsive disorder. Textbook."

This doctor could write prescriptions, which was, of course, what made her a real doctor. She inked the script on a special pad with the name of some pharmaceutical company printed at the top.

On the way to the pharmacy, my father said nothing.

He watched me swallow a pill. Then he said not to get used to doing that for long. It was okay for now but not forever.

Then he said, "Here, drink this."

"Are you a heavyweight yet?"

"Still a lightweight."

Lightweight means that you won't embarrass yourself anymore.

So, roll your sleeves up. Always take any opportunity to do this. In class, act like it's hot in the room and show off the arms. But remember to use clear sports deodorant. Not the flaky, white kind with the aluminum in it. No one wants a snowy forest.

The tub of white powder boasted promises of progress on the wrapper. It didn't mention that it makes your pee cloudy. You can see granules float in the toilet water.

The tub of white powder—one at my father's house and one at my mother's house so that I'd never miss a dose. A collection of empty containers on my desk. Trophies. All showed identical bulging biceps.

My mother said, "Sounds like steroids."

My mother said, "Don't drink that."

A translucent orange pill bottle. **Do not take before driving. Avoid mixing with alcohol. Side effects may vary.** One at my father's house and one at my mother's house so that I'd never miss a dose. My father would watch me from his chair at the kitchen table.

"All wounds heal," he said. "Have you tried the rubber band again? I haven't seen you do the hallway thing in a while. But why do you do that sock thing? You always put a black sock on your right foot and a white sock on your left."

Then he reminded me about the new generation. The neurotic, the hysterical. My mother.

Then he said, "Here, drink this."

You know the rest. So do what I did. You'll need one orange pill bottle and one tub of white powder. Place the pills in a bowl and pound them with the butt of a butter knife—or a butcher's knife. Pour crushed pills into the tub of white powder. Stir.

I said, "Here, drink this."

I said, "I don't think I need the pills anymore."

We clicked our cloudy glasses together.

He asked, "Are you a heavyweight yet?"

The scale said lightweight.

I said, "Welterweight."

A taste like licking wet cement.

BALLADS

At the record store, Greg and I buy Discharge and Darkthrone CDs. We sit in Reiner's room and force him to listen to them.

Greg won't stop talking about this one sound engineer from the studio. The guy used to roadie for Black Flag. Tells a million tour stories. He mixes the music for Greg's band: The Drug Bugs.

Massacre Divine loops over and over on Reiner's boombox. We get high on dry sativa. Then Greg pulls out some coke he got from Kevin. This isn't the good shit Kevin promised, but it's something to burn the time until he scores the high-quality stuff. Each time the record starts over and "City of Fear" roars from the speakers, Greg snorts a line. He gives me some to rub into my gums. It stings and then starts to speed up my thoughts.

I panic. Sliding out the back door and onto the porch, my heart thuds in my ribs.

Later, I brush my teeth until I spit blood into the sink.

Calvin takes Jacqueline and me to the bookstore. Jacqueline gets an Eve Babitz book. She reads the stories and tells us about them. "Eve has some of the wildest stories, and they're all true." She starts calling 280 "The 280" and 80 "The 80." She says, "I hate taking the 101 in the morning. I just stick to the 280."

"You make me want to scream when you do that," Greg says.

We're smoking weed at the skatepark. Our friend, Ken, joins us.

Jacqueline says, "Wilshire Boulevard used to be a road used by the Tongva people. Then these Europeans showed up, changed everything, even the name."

"So obsessed with L.A.," Ken says. "Cliché."

"The Spanish made it look like they invented the road themselves."

Greg says, "This guy at the studio said he watched some dude at this show get punched with a fistful of car keys."

"The Tongva people used to carry tar from La Brea. They took it along what became Wilshire," Jacqueline says. "Scientists keep pulling fossils out of the tar. It's full of thousands of bones."

"Almost lost an eye," Greg says.

"Word," Calvin says.

In the bathroom, near the skatepark, a scrawl on the wall reads, **Kill Emo Posers**. Another reads, **I survived Y2K, and all I got was this lousy skateboard**. In one of the stalls, someone drew a pair of breasts. I used to go to this bathroom and check my testicles for cancer when the OCD got real bad. I'd slip in every day and squeeze around on my balls until they ached and pulsed.

This one time a few weeks back, Greg went into one of the back stalls. He took a big, mega-sized Sharpie and wrote some lyrics against the tile wall. I remember seeing him carefully shape each letter.

Today, I don't check for cancer, but I do go to the back stall and reread Greg's poem.

There's a carnival down the street,
and you say I need to show up cuz they're short a couple freaks.
You held me close up on top of the sheets,
and the loving that you gave me brought me to my knees.
Changes in the weather, trees without leaves,
and I hoped each day you'd show yourself to me.
On the coast and I'm feeling the breeze,
but I know you want my burial at sea.

I leave the stall and stand before the mirror. I stare at myself in the grimy glass, the cavernous gray-cement walls enclose me. The cold riffs of *Transilvanian Hunger* hiss through my headphones. My gums look shrunken and pale, receding from my teeth. This leaves semi-circles of sensitive bone.

I brush my teeth twice when I get home.

I tell Jacqueline my seventh-grade drug has been killing my sex drive. We stand in her blue room.

She plucks dog hair from her fuchsia velour sweatsuit.

"Since I began taking them, I haven't felt much of anything. I told my doctor and she suggested I up the dose."

"Not like you're getting laid," she says.

On her mirror, she taped a picture of herself from middle school. The sunlight in the picture looks bright enough to illuminate the room. Even with the lights switched off, the Polaroid seems to glow.

"You don't get it," I say. "What if I do get laid?"

"Try these first." She opens her sock drawer and snakes her arm around inside. She pulls out an orange bottle and taps out a couple of Gabapentin capsules. "These'll make you horny."

They make me talk a lot.

Calvin, Jacqueline, and I smoke weed at the skatepark until our thumbs crack on the lighter wheel. We get bored and walk over to this retro-style diner. A silky Beach Boys song winds from the loudspeaker. The menus seem a few shades more colorful today. The hot October weekend brings everyone outside, and the Beach Boys ask if "You Still Believe in Me." After standing in line forever, we get shakes and fries.

Calvin dunks his fries in his strawberry milkshake.

"I can't stand when you do that," I say.

We walk over to a nearby park, and Calvin throws the rest of his soggy fries at ducks.

Jacqueline sits cross-legged on the grass, picking daisies. She says, "You know, when you sit on the ground, you're about as tall as a kid. Crazy how they see the world like this all the time." She looks up at the crisscrossing branches, squinting in the sun.

I finish my malt and crush the cup.

"I could never live in Woodside," she says. "If I buy a house, I think I want it to be in Topanga Canyon. I want a Spanish-style. I want land in the Palm Desert."

Calvin starts to hum in a reedy voice.

"Is that Mozart?" I ask.

"Minor Threat."

"Greg likes them," Jacqueline says.

"Where is Greg?" I sit next to her. Calvin drops to the grass, too.

Jacqueline nods towards a group of guys in White Sox jerseys. They cluster around a barbecue pit. "Everyone comes to the Bay trying to get in on the money or the magic or some shit." Her voice sounds distant.

A man in a US Postal Service jersey adjusts the gears on his bike with a small tool. Two people—a man and a woman—sit on a bench, talking. They wear joggers and matching zip-up jackets with the name of some tech-company plastered across the front.

We can't hear what the guys in the White Sox jerseys are saying. We only hear their loud intermittent laughter. A laugh track for a silent film.

Then I realize that none of these people look like they have any exciting stories to tell. They look hollow, and that makes me really scared. No Discharge records or lines of coke to talk about. They look empty. Hourglasses with the sand running out. I realize that I'm sitting here with Jacqueline and Calvin and that I feel so crammed with thoughts that I could burst, but the strangers don't look like they're going to explode—which frightens me—and because they look so empty, they stop looking like real people at all.

Jacqueline interrupts the silence and saves me. "My brother says some slut in his class sucked him off. He said his crotch smelled like watermelon lip gloss for a week. Didn't want to wash it."

The guys in the group laugh hard at something else, and one of them *whoops*. He throws his hat up in the air and catches it.

"I miss being your brother's age," Calvin says. "I used to sit and stare at the drawings of elf wizard ladies in my D&D books for hours."

"Guys are so gross," Jacqueline says. "You know, when I get my license, I want to go for a road trip alone. Take the 5 south until I see nothing but palm trees."

The guys laugh again.

"But first, I'm going to score some pills from Sarah. I've had a lot of panic attacks, and I want a bullet for each of them."

I take my crumpled paper cup to the trash. Aluminum cans and plastic bottles overflow from the top of the bin. A scattering of dirty napkins and paper plates fan out at the base. I find a spot between two bottles and slide my paper cup in without toppling the trash. I stand there, checking one last time to make sure all the built-up garbage doesn't spill out. The delicate position of trash indicates an eventual avalanche. But it looks okay for now.

All okay.

Hours later, the sugar from the shake still clings to my teeth. I brush my teeth until the bristles split from my brush.

I spend several minutes picking the strands off my bleeding gums. In the mirror, I check to make sure I got them all. I notice several bumps on the back of my tongue. The internet tells me that they are normal. But, they may or may not—sometimes but not always—turn cancerous.

All night, I get up and check the bumps in the mirror to make sure they don't look cancerous.

SCAB

Stand up.

Whatever you're doing right now, stop it and stand up.

In a standing position, let your arms hang by your sides. Rotate your palms forward. You should feel your chest open up, your scapulae come together, and your shoulders widen.

Remember this feeling.

This is how your shoulders should look all the time. The palm positioning cues the posterior deltoid muscles. Over time, you'll learn how to achieve this posture with any hand position.

Remember the letter S.

S is for shoulders.

Do several sets of overhead press—military press if you prefer that name. Work until failure. Get big boulder shoulders.

I remember this one guy in sixth grade. He grabbed me by the wrists and shoved me against a wall in the middle of PE class. His big, slightly moist hands gripping my skinny wrists. I tried to resist but felt the promise of injury in his grip.

No one wants to feel like a doll, jerked around.

This kid wore a Gold's Gym lanyard with his house keys clanging. That explained the grip strength.

Sometimes you don't need to fight back—at least not yet. Gauge your odds and come up with a new strategy.

A good defense is a good defense.

They say, with bears, you need to make yourself look as big as possible. Scare the big, dumb idiots away with your posture. They smell your fear or something. Remember, we learned that back on field trips to the Marin Headlands. We'd swing back around the Bay to poke at tide pools.

Anyway, remember S for shoulders and keep them thrust as wide as possible.

Instead of trying to slug it out with that kid, I went home and did dumbbell presses.

If you're still standing, push your chest forward. Take a big breath and inflate your lungs. Push your pecs into place, up and forward. Breathe shallow breaths so that your chest never deflates all the way.

You have many options when bulking this muscle group. You can do several variations of the bench press. Sneak a set of push-ups in whenever you can. Use a cable machine if you have one.

Here's a trick.

Drink lots of water during the day and, when you use the restroom, do a set of push-ups.

Make sure you have a nice bath mat, so that you don't get sick from shit germs. I do it in the hallway for that reason. I don't recommend trying this in the school restrooms.

C is for chest. Don't forget.

We used to have push-up contests in PE. It's easy to cheat, so don't believe anyone's numbers.

In fact, don't compete in those contests at all.

You may think the ladies will like it. You may think you've gotten strong enough to beat the scariest guy.

But when you go down to do push-ups, prepare yourself for some big guy to leap on your back and dry hump you a bunch of times. He'll laughs and snort like a pig.

He's been sent to the office a lot. Except his dad invented some popular tax software, so he's allowed to simulate rape—or something— I guess. They send him back to class, slap on the wrist.

When he gets off of you, calls you a bitch a couple times, and leaves, remember to finish your set.

No one likes sit-ups. If they say they do, they're a fucking liar. So, apologies in advance because I'm telling you that you need to do sit-ups every day.

Build those abdominal muscles. You need to be able to take a punch to the gut. Once you're done with the sit-up set, you can work on the other A, arms. Everyone loves curls.

Curls for girls.

You can do your sets of curls, but only if you do your ab workout first.

With your chest and shoulders in position, you can tighten your abs—belly button to spine—and flex your arms. Squeeze your hands open and closed a few times to get your forearms in action. Pop up all those veins.

This kid knocked me to the ground. I didn't have my abs flexed, so I lost my balance.

The blacktop tore a big chunk from my elbow.

Then he was on me, fists arcing down. You don't forget the way the cement feels on the back of your head. You'll remember the dust in your hair and pebbles grinding into your skull. You don't forget the way a hit to the nose lights your whole face up; you have to suck your air in burning hisses.

You never forget the way they boot you when you're down.

To this day, I can look in the mirror and see the shiny patch where the stretched and itchy scab grew. I don't think he thought about it before going after me. It seemed fun for him to see the skinny kid he hated and knock him down. A few cheap shots.

That's it.

That's the way guys like him seem to think. No deeper motivation.

You can try to figure out why guys do shit like that but spare me. All your theories are probably bullshit and, in the end, theories won't keep you from getting your ass kicked.

Instead, just remember to flex your abs.

I should have. I'd have never lost my balance.

Belly button to spine.

Last, think about your back. If you do enough pull-ups and rows, you can start to see your back from your front. You can spread your muscles and look like a bat or a manta ray. With your shirt off, this will look really impressive. So, I don't care how afraid you are, do your fucking pull-ups every day.

I picked at the red crust where I hurt my arm. That summer, I did my pull-ups and squats and curls and push-ups. Bent over rows, hammer curls, military press, and chest press. Cable pulls, face pulls, pull-downs...

BaRefOOT

Calvin tells me he went to a doctor about his insomnia. The doctor gave him a prescription for boring science-fiction books. He told Calvin the books cure all kinds of insomnia and restlessness.

Calvin runs his finger along a shelf of old paperbacks.

"You looking for anything in particular?"

"Yeah, an eraser," he says.

"The fuck is that?" I sit down on a dirty step-stool in the aisle. The movement pushes air and my cologne up into my nostrils. Really covers up the smell of dust. The only other sound in the store is the careful shifting of other shoppers.

"I've thought about it a while," he says. He pulls out a book by Octavia Butler and reads the back. Then he sets the book back on the shelf. "Looks too interesting."

"You said erasers?"

"Oh, yeah." He turns to look at me. "You remember the year your parents split?"

I tell him that I do.

He gets me to pull out other images. I swim back in my memories to the day my parents had a big fight. Mom and Dad book-ended the kitchen. My mom sat cross-legged on the linoleum, head back against the silverware drawer. My dad stood, propped on the counter opposite her. They kept screaming over a sea of white tile. I still don't know what happened in the moments before I entered the room, but something hung in the air between them like the ozone after a thunder strike.

That day, I walked over to Calvin's house. Didn't put shoes on—not sure why I forgot them. That was during the time of year when the rough blacktop burns your soles. You gotta walk on your heels and step on the shadows.

Anyway, he brought a bucket so that I could wash my feet clean. Then we ate Costco cheese-puffs and coated the PlayStation controllers orange.

I ask him, "So what?"

And he tells me, "Think about that fight but without the cheese-puffs. Think of the screams and scenes in the kitchen. Now, what if that's where your mind lives, forever. You can't hold on to your good memories; you always go right back to the fights and screaming. How do you get rid of those images?"

This is where I shrug.

"Yeah." He crouches down to check out the bottom shelf.

"But what does it mean that you're looking for erasers?"

"Well." He stands up. "That stuff down there looks too boring." He shakes his head then looks at me. "Any suggestions?"

"Just answer my question. I've asked you like twenty times." I stand up and look at the shelf. "What *are* erasers? Can..." I squint, "Philip K. Dick erase things?"

"He has a lot of stories about memory."

I just stare at him, waiting.

"You've got medicine for your OCD," he says. "You've found your erasers. Like all those thoughts you talk about. Your medicine helps erase them, right? I need my own erasers. I need to erase the memories."

"Okay?" I say it as a question. "What memories?"

"You should understand better than anyone," he says. "We all need erasers."

"Yeah, I guess." I shake my head. "The medicine is whatever. Not sure if it really works. Also, what memories?"

He keeps digging through titles. "I didn't think finding a book would be this difficult. Also, I've read all those Philip K. Dick books."

I lean against one of the shelves. "You coming to Jacqueline's party?"

"You can go ahead of me," he says. "I'll stay here a bit. I need to make an entrance, right?"

"Sure, yeah."

I leave Calvin at the book store and walk to Jacqueline's place. It takes eight songs on shuffle to get there. A few drops of rain start to fall, and the world smells briefly wonderful.

Jacqueline answers the door. "You're so fucking early."

At her shin, her dog peaks its nose between her leg and the doorframe.

"I mean, I can come back later."

"No, come in."

In the kitchen, a box of Heineken sits on the counter. Stacks of letters, junk mail, bills, and magazines look near collapse. Dried ramen noodles stick to the stone countertops like dead worms on hot cement. The smell of sweet weed smoke lingers in the air.

Jaqueline takes me upstairs. "You'll have to watch me get ready."

In her bedroom, she sits in front of her vanity.

She picks out a makeup brush. "I can't wait to see Sarah. I haven't seen her in ages."

"She hot?" I sit on the bed.

"You're so disgusting." She sets the brush down. "You threw me off. I didn't need that one." She picks up a bottle of concealer and unscrews the cap.

"Huh?" Light from outside cuts turquoise lines through the blinds.

"Sarah is pretty, though," Jacqueline says. "Super rich. Lives in some Atherton mansion."

"You're rich, too."

"Kind of." She starts applying patches of concealer over pimple scars. "My mom has Menlo Park money. Her parents have Atherton money. You know what I mean?"

"Sure," I say.

"Weird house, though." She dips the brush back into the concealer bottle then applies a few more daubs.

"What do you mean?" I look down. "Also, can I take my shoes off?"

She turns to look at me and squints, a quick headshake to indicate a question.

"They're dirty."

A loud sigh. "Yeah, whatever."

I slide my shoes off and push them under her bed. "Her house," I prompt. "You were saying."

"Oh, yeah. My dad—before he moved out—he used to drive me around in the Lexus you see out front."

"Before his Lambo?"

"Yes, before his Lambo." She dabs her face with a tan sponge. "He might have to sell that Lambo, though. Hard times, right? Anyway, he drove me in the Lexus and pointed out all the types of houses. I got to know all the names for them. California ranch, mid-century, Victorian, Continental, modern, Eichler. Though that last one is also kind of a mid-century."

"What the fuck is a mid-century?"

"That's not the point. Let me get to the point," Jacqueline says, gesturing at me with the sponge. She sets it down, then picks up a flat brush and a squeeze tube.

"What is your point?"

"I got really good at spotting different houses." She squeezes something opaque and brownish onto the brush like toothpaste. "But when I went to Sarah's house, I kept trying to figure out what kind of house it was."

"Could be one you've never heard of." I shrug.

She brushes a layer of the paste onto her face. "No," she says. "This is my dad's business. He's not worth shit. But he does know what he's talking about with houses. Driving with him was like listening to someone read a phonebook. He named houses and clipped his toenails in the living room. That was my dad. Except he'd just clip the corner of each toenail then tear across the nail. That leaves a strip of sensitive pink skin showing. Used to watch him do it. I guess just to freak myself out." She visibly shudders. "Either that or I wanted to see the most sensitive part of him: that little sliver."

I interrupt. "So, what was with Sarah's house?"

"Oh, yeah. You ever get a word on the tip of your tongue, and you try to find it, but it's like someone deleted it from your mind?" She sets down the brush and selects another. There's a flat tub that she uncaps. "That's how I felt the whole party. I kept thinking, *It's a... it's a...* But couldn't finish the thought. Couldn't figure it out." She pats the brush into the tub, and powder floats into the air like motes of dust. She begins patting it against her cheeks.

"Maybe you aren't as good at identifying houses as you thought you were."

"No, I'm good at it," she says. "You remember when we ground up NoDoz pills and snorted lines?"

"Oh, fuck."

She laughs. "That's what not finding the word felt like. You bug your eyes out after a line. You want to have a thought. To think about what just happened. But you can't have a thought when it feels like someone stuck a lighter up your nose." She sets down the powder and pushes it aside. Several palettes of eye makeup lie open, displaying rows of shining gradients.

"So that's the weird house story?" I ask. "You went to a pool party with Sarah and got confused?"

"Yeah," she says. "It bothered me a lot. You know?"

"No," I say.

"Anyway," Jacqueline says, "Sarah's bringing Charlotte with her. Charlotte's been like, 'It's going to be so nice to see you, Jackie' —I hate when people call me Jackie —and all these questions. 'Are you still with Greg?' 'What are you going to wear?' Shit like that."

"What *are* you going to wear?" Several outfits lay across the bed next to me.

"Why do you care so much? Weird." She shuts an eye-shadow palette and digs through a cup full of mascara wands.

"It was, like, something to ask," I say.

She does her mascara and then applies a lip-liner. Then she turns to me. "Do I look good?"

"Yeah." I sit up a little. "I mean, doesn't it matter what Greg thinks the most?"

She tilts her head to the side and creases her brow. "But I'm asking you."

"Yeah, you look good." My face feels too hot.

"Fuckable?"

My dry tongue sticks to the roof of my mouth. I don't say anything.

"I'll take that as a yes," she says and turns back to her mirror.

My tongue makes a cracking sound as I peel it off my palette. "Sure."

"Good." She puts her face right up to the mirror and squints. "Also, I need to change. Go to the bathroom and fix your hair. It looks like shit."

When I stand up, she says, "Fuck. It's October. Shoulda chosen Halloween colors for the eye makeup."

After I fix my hair, Reiner arrives. He picks up Jacqueline's dog and carries it around. We stand in the living room as Jacqueline straightens couch cushions.

"Where the fuck is Greg?" Reiner says, holding the dog a few inches from his knit sweater.

"Smoking with Ken or something," Jacqueline says. She turns to me. "FYI, you asked what I was wearing. Hudson Jeans and a Hollister top."

"Charlotte was the one who wanted to know," I say.

Reiner rolls his eyes. "Charlotte," he says in a breathy voice and shakes his head. Then he looks at my feet. "Your socks don't match."

Heavy shoes stomp up the steps, and the front door opens. The doorway frames Greg and Ken, rain-wet hair stuck to their foreheads. Behind them, lavender wilts in the planter boxes along the porch.

"Don't track mud inside," Jacqueline says.

Greg starts kicking his feet against the doormat, scraping off mud. Ken strips off his hoodie. His form-fitting cotton tee shows off all the muscle he built in the gym last summer. Greg wears a boxy button-up that makes him look like a kid wearing his father's clothes.

"Hey," Greg says, "Calvin not with you?"

"Said he wants to make an entrance or something."

"He's fucking weird," Reiner says.

"He's not bad," Jacqueline says, waving her hand at Reiner. "Cut him some slack."

"Yeah, Calvin's cool," I say.

"That's because you two have a weird friendship," Ken says, laughing. "Everyone's like, 'Get married already.'"

There's a painful kick in my stomach, so I squeeze my abs tight. I start to roll back my shoulders. My forearms contract. SCAB out of order feels so wrong.

"I'm trying to smoke," Greg says.

"Wait until Charlotte and Sarah arrive," Jacqueline says.

"Charlotte's that anorexic one, right?" Ken asks.

"Yeah." Reiner sets the dog down. "It's so obvious she does it for attention."

"Come on." Jacqueline gives Reiner a light hit on the arm. "Charlotte goes through a lot. She used to come over last year. She'd eat nothing but pickles."

Greg laughs.

"She had to go to the hospital last year," Jacqueline says.

"Even better way to get attention," Reiner says.

Ken and Greg laugh.

Jacqueline says, "I heard Sarah started selling pills, and I'm going to need one after dealing with you idiots. Don't fuck it up for me."

We find seats in the living room and open beers. After a while, two girls arrive—one brunette and one redhead. The brunette smiles and hugs Jacqueline. The smile shows little teeth in a pinched bird's face. Next, the redhead hugs Jacqueline.

"So glad to see you," Jacqueline says. When they break the embrace, Jacquline turns to the rest of us. "This is Sarah"—the redhead—"and Charlotte"—the brunette—Jacqueline says.

Charlotte wears Levis and a shirt that reads, *Shhh... I'm dreaming.* Hair chopped into a bob. Shoes like a ballerina might dance in.

Sarah rocks a tie-side dress with a loud floral print. Deep V-neck to show off her cleavage. Black boots laced up to her mid-shin. Thick red hair crowds half her face. A clip-in feather dangles by her left cheek.

Reiner slips into a low voice. "How do you do, ladies?" He makes an exaggerated wink. He gets their faces rosy with laughter.

Ken passes around a Technicolor, hand-blown pipe. The mouthpiece glistens with spit. Beer-breath and lip gloss all smear together. It's like kissing everyone in the room at once.

I cough out my hit, sputter, then sprint into the bathroom, head dizzy. Something like a chunk of lung swirls down the drain. I blow my nose and toss the Kleenex into the trash bin. The tissue lands on top of several pieces of colorful stationery. Someone folded each paper up into a neat rectangle. I pull one of them out and unfold it on the marble countertop. Technicolor dolphins break from an inviting sea, whipping their tails in a soothing sunset, forever. I haven't seen stationary like this since elementary school. The vague shapes of words wind across the page. Someone had written something on it then erased it. When I hold up the message to the light, I can read the line: **I don't know why you keep bailing on me. I can't help but think that you're more interested in someone else.**

The rest looks too faded, so I fold them up and toss them back into the trash. The whole experience feels wrong, like finding a dildo in your parents' dresser.

Back in the living room, everyone watches me enter. Ken exhales a cloud of smoke.

Reiner puts a hand on my shoulder. Sing-song, he says, "It's okay to be a pussy—like me."

Charlotte laughs and touches Reiner's elbow.

"Dude, you're so high," I say.

"Dude, you're so high," Greg says to me. "As they say, 'Cough to get off.'"

Greg and Jacqueline sit on the couch, cuddle-close to each other. Sarah sits on an armchair. Charlotte and Ken hover around the mantle.

Jacqueline says, "What have you been up to, Sarah? Feels like forever since that pool party."

"Oh, not much," Sarah says. She looks over at me then back to Jacqueline. "College applications."

"I feel you," Jacqueline says. "Greg can't even prep for the SATs without Ritalin."

"What?" Greg asks, paying attention now.

Sarah leans forward to speak. "I've heard it all before." She looks around the room. "Parents planning your careers while you're still in daycare. No wasted seconds. Be careful though. When you streamline living, that's when you die young."

"Oh, yeah," Jacqueline nods. "But like, I've been looking for Xanax for a minute. Nobody has them anymore."

"Not at all," Charlotte says. "Right, Sarah?"

"Xanex was so ninth grade," Sarah says. "No one has them anymore. The only way that anyone gets them is if their doctor gives them to you. Doctors start you with SSRIs, anyway."

"Wait," Jacqueline says. She laughs in a louder voice than usual. "How do you know?"

Sarah smiles and nods. "Hey, I know how it is. Everyone wants Xanax, Ativan, Klonopin. It's because we're all fucked up and stressed."

"Tell me about it," Reiner says. Then he points to me. "He's had stress-induced constipation for a decade."

That's when SCAB kicks in. "Fuck you, dude," I say.

"It's okay," Jacqueline says. She waves her hand at me. "That's not the point. But anyway, I guess I'll keep looking around and trying to find it."

"You know," Sarah says. Then she pauses and looks at me, tilting her head up like she's thinking.

Jacqueline leans forward, and she opens and closes her hands once.

"I may be able to find something for you," Sarah says. "I help friends out. If they're there for me, then I find things for them."

"Oh, she'll be there if pills are involved," Reiner says. "Jacqueline will even give you a spot in her Top Eight spaces."

"Reiner," Jacquline says, but she stops. She looks at him. Her crinkled nose makes a washboard. The music plays a few beats.

"So how 'bout them Niners?" Charlotte says.

Sarah laughs.

"They suck," Ken says. "Same as every year."

"Who wants shots?" Charlotte asks.

We all take shots and break off into groups. Somehow, I end up sitting next to Sarah on the couch. Jacqueline starts playing Fall Out Boy at a deafening volume. "Sugar, We're Going Down" is her and Greg's song ("This one makes me think of you, babe"). So, Sarah has to lean close to hear me.

I tell her something stupid, but simple enough. About the year I started lifting weights because I didn't feel big enough. And that was at a rec center down the street from me. This girl from class worked out there who didn't feel fit enough either. Funny enough, that girl was Jacqueline.

She tells me that's cool, but she and Jacqueline met at summer camp. They used to run around the camp pool, letting their feet slap on the patio. Then she tells me that, even if it's dark in here, my eyes still look beautiful.

I don't know what to do, so I sit there and tense up and flex my chest muscles for some reason.

Then she breaks the tension and asks me more.

Time slips away in the living room.

Over the music, Jacqueline starts shouting.

Sarah rolls her eyes and stands up to follow the sound.

Everyone gathers in the kitchen.

Jacqueline and Greg face each other.

Ken stands in the background, looking disinterested, taking another hit from the pipe.

"You can't say that," Jacqueline says.

"It's a joke," Greg says.

That's when Jacqueline picks up a stack of junk mail, energy bills, and fashion magazines. She hurls the pile at Greg.

He puts up an arm and ducks a rain of blow-ins and perfume samples and coupons and exclusive deals.

"I can't talk over this crap," Sarah says next to my ear. Her hot breath puckers my skin in the most addictive way.

We head out front.

"I don't have my shoes," I say.

"Who cares?" Sarah says.

My socks soak up water from the brick walkway that leads from the front porch to the driveway. A light sprinkle taps the top of my head. After the loud music inside, my ears feel full of cotton.

"Let's check her car," Sarah says, big smile on her face. She takes my hand and leads the way.

I pull open the back door and the dome-light flips on.

"What the fuck?" Sarah stumbles backward.

I reach out and catch her.

The tail-end of her dress rakes against a puddle.

Once she has her footing, we turn to the back seat.

"Oh, shit," I say, laughing.

Calvin sits up, wiping his eyes. The book he had spread open on his chest topples into his lap.

"Oh, sorry dude," he says.

"What the fuck are you doing in there?"

Sarah laughs, "You know him?"

"Yeah."

"Okay, still kind of weird, dude," she says to Calvin. Then she looks up at me. "Raincheck?"

"Yeah."

She smiles then turns. Her boots click up the path back to the house.

"Way to fuck it up for me," I say. "The fuck were you doing?"

He sits up all the way and rotates until he's facing the front seat. I slide in next to him.

"I got here a while ago. Wasn't sure if I wanted to join yet. I needed the right moment to make an entrance. I checked her car. Unlocked."

"Only someone in Menlo Park would leave their car unlocked."

"Yeah, well, I fell asleep."

We laugh.

"Dude," I say, "Jacqueline and Greg started fighting. Plus, thanks to you, I'm not going to get laid tonight."

"Sorry, dude."

"I'll get my shoes, then I'm heading home. Want to walk with me?"

"Yeah." He wipes the last of the sleep from his eyes. Then he laughs. He says, "Well, that doctor was right. The book *did* work."

IN LAS VEGAS ON THE DAY OF ARMAGEDDON

When some apocalyptic war wipes us all out, and—with no ozone—the sun cooks the earth's crust, all the pools in Las Vegas will empty. Nothing but bone-dry concrete bowls and Armageddon silence.

Sounds like a great place to skate.

Our skatepark in Menlo Park looks a little like that. Except no acid rain and, when it does rain, you end up with little puddles at the bottom of the bowls. No silence, either. All chatter and competing boomboxes. No casinos, but the gamblers all find their way to Silicon Valley eventually.

You hear things. Like this one girl, she fucks this grad student who helps her with her AP calc homework. Her parents heard rumors.

You can guess what they did.

The grad student will get her into Stanford or Cal, but a pregnancy won't. So, they bought their girl condoms.

There's this other chick, her dad's a marketing executive. She spells out messages on the ground in multi-colored masking tape. She calls it transient art because it only lasts a day or two.

She writes: **Abandon Ship!**

Kevin skates with anyone. If you approach him to teach you a trick, there isn't a trick he can't show you.

He sometimes dates a girl named Lore. She dyed her hair so often that now all she has left is fried gray grandma hair. Next year, when she's a senior in high school, she better fix it or the jokes will never end.

The tape girl spells out a new message in red and black: **Who's next?**

These two football players who bus to our school from East Palo Alto like to chill at the park on Fridays before game day. They wear button-down shirts, black slacks, and ties. You can smell the spray deodorant wafting off them.

They sit on benches in dappled autumn light, scraping up chow mein and sweet-and-sour chicken from Styrofoam containers. The football players don't skate, but they chill here because the pigs don't harass crowds of CEO children.

Sometimes people disappear. They go to rehab or something. When parents don't know what to do with their kids, they ship them off to programs in Joshua Tree where they have to survive in the desert and start their own fires like Jack London. We all call it "getting sent to wilderness."

When some apocalyptic war begins, no one will believe it until a mushroom-cloud balloons over their backyard, but at least some of us will know how to start a fire with flint and steel.

A guy with pink highlighter streaks in his hair hands out what look like baseball cards. Each card features a naked woman. Little lens flares obscure pussies, nipples, and assholes. Printed across the tops of the cards are phone numbers with Las Vegas area codes. He says he found them in his dad's office.

He gives me a card, which tells me that I can spend the night with a beautiful blonde named Kim for the cost of a fancy dinner.

Lore with the gray hair combs out knots on a bench. Wispy, chemical-killed strands float away.

None of the people here can touch their trust funds until they're 21. A favorite game to play is to fantasize about what you'll buy when you can finally get your hands on all that money. Like people who buy lottery scratchers or shoot craps do.

On the day of Armageddon, the stock markets will collapse. What's left of the icebergs will wash up with upended crabs on a beach near you.

Kevin says, "The craziest thing my dad ever did was when he got married and didn't sign a prenup. I guess being an engineer doesn't make you very smart."

Ken meets a girl named Jasmine. She wears draping cardigans and Sharpies her nails black. Red streaks dash through her dark, curly hair. A week later, Ken and Jasmine hold hands and fuck around together behind the bathrooms.

Some kid ODs. A guy we barely knew. That's what they call it on the local paper at least: **an OD**. Like it was by mistake or he was just partying too hard, they said it was an accident. Except he took the entire bottle of Xanax his doctor gave him. They say OD. Even though he'd taken the drug for years and knew the doses.

A campaign marches around downtown Menlo Park, chanting about the dangers of recreational drug use. You can see their bright white shirts and clipboards. They'll warn you about the risks of ending up like the dead kid. They say, "Why risk an overdose?"

No one really wants to talk about why he took them all. After it happened, his parents kind of withdrew, people stopped hearing from them much.

Dying from Xanax is supposed to relax your muscles to the point that they cease working. Your lungs and heart sort of cave in on themselves. Someone at the skatepark says that the dead guy "chilled out to death."

Kevin screams aloud to anyone that'll listen. He says it's always the parents' fault. When he gets like this, his eyes take on a different look. A look like he's an unfamiliar dog who may act in any number of unpredictable ways.

You get the sense that we're all just waiting around for the day of Armageddon. Kids here talk about the ice caps, the ozone hole, aerosols, and dying polar bears. Kids blast Megadeth and Suicidal Tendencies songs from speakers. Like a little cult that can't wait for the day of Armageddon, so that they can have one last big "I told you so" before disintegrating into sand.

Greg and Jacqueline sit together on the edge of a skating bowl. They hold hands and lean on one another.

"Babe?" Jacqueline says.

"Yeah, babe?" Greg says back.

"We gotta get through high school, stay together through college—depending where we go—find jobs near each other, hope we don't grow apart, then make marriage work."

Greg sits there and rubs his chin, feeling for incoming stubble. He says, "Damn, you make 'I'll love you forever,' sound like winning an Olympic gold."

The tape girl spends an hour using every color of tape on her latest project. She writes: **All Art is Transient Art and Even Languages Die.**

"That's my best work yet," she says. "Wish I could save it."

In Las Vegas, on the day of Armageddon, the black-tinted casino windows will mean that gamblers will be the last to know.

There, you will find us, dipping into the dead swimming pools, trying to master the Front Slide Disaster.

SARAH

Every night, propped up with pillows in my bed, I exchange instant messages with Sarah.

She tells me an *au pair* used to take care of her.

I ask her what an *au pair* is.

She says it's like a nanny. Except they're from France or Spain or Germany—her *au pair* came from Germany.

I tell her that I had a nanny from Colombia, and does that count?

She says probably not.

At school, I talk with Calvin about erections. About how scared I am of not getting one. "What if Sarah wants to fuck and my meds make it hard to get hard?" I ask.

"Remember your ABCs," he says.

Sarah says her dad made her take a road trip to visit colleges. "He has a Land Rover for things like that."

When I ask if the trip was fun, she says, "Most of this country sickens me."

I ask her if she feels the same way about California.

She says, "Do you think someone could live off nothing but gas station food?"

A is for apple. This should be easy to remember. Shoot for this hardness. You want the head to pulse. She will feel the difference.

"My dad likes to fuck these young foreign women," Sarah says. "He has a mistress or something in Cupertino. She just moved here."

"Your mom know?" I ask.

"I think it's the accents," she says. "They can't speak English very well. That way, he can feel like a conqueror. You know?"

"Your brother know?"

"Anyway," she says. "I think I'm the only person who likes hazelnut creamer."

B stands for banana. Think of it with the peel removed. How you can shake it, and it won't bend. It isn't apple-hard, but you can work with bananas. They can get the job done.

"My favorite college has the same name as me. Sarah Lawrence," she says. "Except, you know, my last name isn't Lawrence."

"Where's that?"

"Yonkers."

"Where's that?"

Sarah sends me a picture of her. She wears an emerald green top that gives me a good view of her breasts.

"You're beautiful," I say.

"What do you think about me studying social work?" she asks.

"Sorry," I say. "I was looking at you."

She sends me another picture. This time, she reclines on a sofa. She wears a lacy bra and a black miniskirt. Tan stockings cling to her legs. High heels, the color of cartoon hearts with stiletto tips.

"I bet I could be great at it," she says.

"You're so hot."

"I could figure out everyone's problems," she says.

"I can't stop looking at you."

She sends a third photo. Same couch and outfit. But nipples, the color of carnations, pop from the top of the bra.

"They have such a great program," she says.

"You make me want to cum."

"Okay," she says. "But, like, I bet no one would fuck with me. Not when I have my degree. There is no shortage of fucked up kids in the world. All those poor people who don't know how to parent."

"Yeah," I say. My penis pulses in my pants. It throbs against the bottom of the laptop—hardness level at A. "You know, you could make great money being a psychiatrist. Jacqueline wants to do something similar. Maybe the two of you could talk about it." By talk about it, I just imagine the two of them making out.

"Makes sense," she says. "Aren't you going to masturbate to me?" She sends a topless photo. In it, she bites the tip of her finger.

I grab lotion. When I touch myself, it really feels like an apple.

"I want you to say my name out loud when you cum," she says. "Promise me you will."

I keep my promise in a quivering voice. "You're so hot," I say and wipe myself up with a dirty pair of boxers.

"I know."

C stands for candle. They burn fast but flame out and start to get soft.

One night, while we're talking, Sarah tells me that she had this pool party over the summer.

She had a lot to say, and I'm probably not doing the story justice the way I tell it, but anyway, this is how it went.

Sarah woke that day with the heat pounding in her head. She slipped out of sweaty sheets and moved to the pool patio, the hot flagstones cooking a crust onto the soles of her feet. She uncorked one of several champagne bottles that she'd chilled overnight in the guesthouse fridge—some big, silver, two-door high-wattage monster that could fit a couple of us standing with our hands stretched above our heads. No parents in the main house. They'd left her with one of their credit cards Scotch-taped to the—even larger—fridge that hummed almost noiselessly in the main kitchen.

The credit card and her fake ID let Sarah load up on drinks: She hates any beer that isn't *light* and all forms of brown liquor. Picture the fridge stuffed with a bunch of pool water beers and girly drinks—flavored vodka and all that.

Charlotte showed up around the time Sarah had washed the heat hangover out of her skull with icy water. Sarah showed Char her plans. Greg and Ken's band was going to play. I'd forgotten they'd done this gig. Jacqueline said she tried to invite me, but this must have been when I was locking myself up in my room or something and being a shut-in.

The plan was to be pretty careful. No need to trash the house or bring everyone in the neighborhood down on them. Money gets you a lot of things, but people in Atherton keep things buttoned up and buttoned down. Can't have the daughters of business popping up in the local paper to embarrass the family.

"We talked about girl stuff while we set everything up," Sarah says. "I was ducking my ex at the time. You wouldn't care."

People showed up on foot, and the girls poured everyone drinks. Shot glasses left little rings of clear liquor all over the tables. Sarah fished silver and blue beer cans out of ice chests and buckets.

"Everything was going great."

Enough people gathered in the yard for a little buzz of conversation to start up: all bullshitting and flirting. Then Greg, Jacqueline, and Ken stopped by, Greg and Ken dragging amplifiers and hard guitar cases. Even Kevin made an appearance, clustering with a couple of smokers around the back fence, wearing black boots and waving his smoke away with his hands. He even passed Sarah a couple things—coke mostly and a couple downers to take the edge off.

Sarah says that this was the moment she started fucking up. She says throwing a party is a double-edged sword. It means you don't have to buy any drugs because people lay them at your feet. All you need is enough alcohol to get things started.

In the guesthouse, people drank beers and kicked their dirt-coated feet up on the Restoration Hardware. Charlotte poured Sarah and herself shots then the two of them took lines of coke off the granite countertop. Sarah says she hit the lines so hard, it was like she ripped the powder right off the stone—and there she was, Sarah, her hair pouring down her back, the world opening up, all her subjects gathered around her, an endless flow of money at the tips of her lacquered nails, and everyone salivated, intent on kissing her feet and dangling from her every word, the party pulsing in this yard, where music swelled up in waves and, from above, grasping rays of sunlight bathed her, bathed and lapped at every inch of her skin, making her silk-soft and glowing—they would tell tales of Sarah and those that had used her before would never dare dream of that again—she would never worry what any of them could ever do to stop her, so long as she uncovered the secrets contained in that single second of unfathomable, ecstatic, orgiastic bliss.

That's when the party started swirling. The way a bunch of people dancing in a backyard turns into something metaphysical. Greg's band kicked off, and Sarah swears she could see the music flowing through the air. A few partiers slipped into the main house. Through a great bay window, she could see the drunks throwing themselves against the plush sofas and resting their beers on coffee tables. Through the glass, with the low afternoon sunlight— which reflected an image of the party outside—the trespassers in the living room took on a blurry cast like the way you remember a dream.

The band banged out rhythms which bounced against the back of the house. The snare slaps and their momentary reverberations went in and out of phase, a grinding guitar saw-toothing through her head. Sarah could see Jacqueline there at the front, where a semi-circle curved around the epicenter of racket. All partiers holding their drinks aloft. Above them, soft clouds moved across the purest blue, that hue that wrapped Sarah's heart in rest and, in the tips of her fingers, she felt a sort of buzzing, like she had the power to reach into the sky and enfold herself in it.

That's what she said at least. I think she's trying to sound poetic. Anyway, after that, things got a lot different.

Greg's band had the stamina for like five songs, then they needed a beer break. When their amps shut off, snuffing a lingering cry of distortion, there was momentary silence. No music to slip into the gaps. Conversation seemed to cease. In a collective inhalation, everyone felt a screeching self-consciousness and, the longer the lull lasted, the tighter this tension wound. At last, Sarah fumbled something onto the speaker, and a song—maybe it was Deftones' "My Own Summer"—came on and saved them all.

Greg and Ken slid inside, chasing the next round of shots.

Sarah tried to spot Jacqueline out of the crowd. From her position by the pool, Sarah could see lights flickering on and off in the upstairs windows. Then he stepped out of the dark. A total kick in the stomach.

A buzz of fear at the bottom of her spine. Her ex smiled and struck out his hand, placing his palm on the ridge of bone right between her breasts, pushing her backwards, backwards, backwards...

Losing her equilibrium, the world went spinning, the cold water seeming to reach up from the pool, still cold because Sarah—stupid, stupid, stupid—in all her hurried preparations hadn't remembered to turn the heat back on for the summer—so much like her mother, who her father said could never do things right—and now that freezing water soaked into her clothing, making it heavy and sucking her down, and with her head dropping beneath the surface, some of that same cold water shooting into her nostrils, burning worse than the coke, her eyes filling, same chlorine burn, the sky above going all blurry in slow motion, the weight of her clothing gradually increasing and taking her towards the bottom, and before the surface could clear up, here they came, cascading over the edge—runners when the starting pistol fires—some of them still in their clothing, overcome by their wilder impulses, others having the composure to strip down first, their windmilling legs, the subsonic booms of broken surface tension as they dove one by one into the blue, and before Sarah reached the bottom, before she twisted her feet underneath her, before she pushed off, before she jetted to the surface, breaking through to suck in the evening air, before any of that, while she was still drifting towards the bottom of the pool, watching her friends swim, she thought that they all looked momentarily happy and that that alone was beautiful.

When she dragged herself onto the lip of the pool, her clothes heavy with water, she realized that the party had passed her ability to control it, and the people now streaming through the sliding door into her living room, these strange people—she could tell—didn't even recognize her, so why would they listen if she told them to chill out and not wreck the place? She turned back to face the patio, and some people outside—a few of them still wet—seemed to follow her, rushing past her, and slipping through the sliding-glass door, flooding inside (and dripping!) into the living room.

Flipping back to the staircase, a couple people began climbing to the second floor, their voices and laughter echoing in the stairwell.

Her heart raced. Flitting about, trying to quell her guests, Sarah felt like she was trying to press blood back inside a wound.

"Hey, Sarah." Ken reached out of the crowd and stood next to her. "I saw your ex a second ago."

"Yeah, I know." Sarah pushed through the door. In the kitchen, people were tearing open packages of food from the pantry. Sarah had kicked her shoes off at the door, and now she could feel crunched up chips and sticky soda clinging to her feet.

That's when Sarah started to run, pushing past people, rounding the bottom of the stairs and pumping her legs up every step.

At the top of the stairs, a lanky guy sprawled on the floor, his sweaty hair laying drooped on the carpet. Sarah stepped over him and down the hall. All the lights switched off, but she knew the way.

She pressed open the door to her bedroom, sucking in the day-old spurts of her perfume that still hung in the air. The relief of aromas: her clothes and her pillow sweat. The animalistic desire for a den. The cocaine wearing off and her dopaminergic delirium fading, Sarah began to exhale. The figure skittered off the bed, tumbling out of view, just the last flash of a pale leg in the slits of light through the blinds and, jerking up in bed, an age-old friend, Charlotte, grasping at the comforter to cover her chest.

I type a single-word response, **Dafuq?**

"Yeah, I was pissed. I let the party go on a bit, then I screamed everyone off the property. You should hear how loud I can be."

"But, wait? Why was Charlotte in your bed?"

"Don't you mean, *with* who?"

"Yeah, I guess."

"Let me just say that I don't think Jacqueline would want to know."

Combine D and E. Flip them around, and you get ED. That's what you never ever want. Life-over. You might as well drop off the face of the earth.

Sarah says, "Let's have dinner this weekend. My place."

"Sure."

START-UP

The train rolls into the station and we board.

Jacqueline throws herself down on a bench seat in one of the booths. "He's late. Late for my birthday."

I sit on the bench opposite her. Charlotte squeezes in beside Jacqueline and Calvin beside me.

"It's all right." Charlotte clicks her nails together. "We're getting drinks with my friend first. He can catch the next one."

The train starts the steady grind, picking up momentum.

"More like the train after that." Jacqueline crosses her arms.

San Francisco showcases summer weather in late October. Though, as it is San Francisco, the weather still feels like a Los Angeles winter.

The city gleams. One can see the concrete sides of Candlestick Park rising from the hillside. The arena perches there like a crow's nest overlooking Daly City.

We brush past commuters onto the cement platform. Silver and red trains jet past in either direction. The hazy blue sky stretches above.

A yellow cab plucks us from the curb and shuttles us toward the Yerba Buena neighborhood.

We slide to a stop before a shining tower that stabs upwards from a sea of concrete. The cab leaves us out front, and we enter the lobby.

A translucent elevator arrives and then drags us up the building.

"Don't look down," Calvin says as the city shrinks to miniature below us.

We reach our stop and walk across hard-packed carpets that smell of detergent. At the end of a sterile hallway, Charlotte bangs on a cream-colored door.

A wiry man with a dark shadow of a beard opens up and waves us inside. "Glad you could make it," he says. "Brennon." He has rock-climber callouses on his palm and a handshake to match.

I slip into SCAB.

For Jacqueline and Charlotte, he offers hugs.

Brennon takes us into a flat white living room. Wall-length windows form a corner, offering a panoramic view of San Francisco.

A second man sits on a pale sofa in a puffer vest and a pair of slacks. His receding, peach hairline leaves a shiny semicircle above his forehead.

A young woman sits beside him, her eyes lost in some dreamy murk. She's skinny—totally hot—wearing a glimmering metallic top. Her straight raven hair, parted down the center, hangs on either side of her face.

"Meet Floyd," Brennon says, "a.k.a. 'the Woz 2.0.'" Brennon struts over and high-fives Floyd. The slap echoes in the hard room.

"Greetings," Floyd says, turning to the rest of us.

"This is Sarah's brother," Charlotte says, gesturing to Floyd.

"My little sister won't even come visit me," he says and laughs. "Always too busy for me. But tell her, for everything I get for her, she could stop by."

Brennon looks out the window. "Your sister is weird, dude."

"Sure," Charlotte says, following Brennon's gaze, taking in the city below. The double-pane glass mutes the scenery. "Nice digs, by the way."

"Fuck yeah," Brennon says. He turns and sits down, draping his arms over the back of the couch.

"Five figs a month," Floyd adds.

Jacqueline eyes the woman. "Who's she?"

"Oh, that's Tomi," Floyd says. "Don't worry about her."

Brennon fidgets, then stands up. "Drinks," he says, then claps. He slides behind the bar in the corner and plucks down a bottle of rum. A row of shot glasses stands in a line along the top of the counter. "Char," Brennon says, "tell your bro to get on this shit. We're getting hot." He pours the rum, careful not to let the glasses overflow.

"Recession-proof, baby," Floyd says from the couch. "Like the fucking Sopranos, man."

"Oh, cool." Charlotte nods.

"Who the fuck are these guys?" Calvin whispers to me.

I shrug.

"So, who's the birthday girl?" Floyd asks, standing up.

"Me," Jacqueline says, hands clasped together at her waist. "Sweet sixteen."

Floyd walks over to her, arms outstretched. "Birthday hug."

She allows it.

Brennon takes one of the shot glasses and presents it to Jacqueline. He passes out the remaining shots.

We all toast and take sips of our rum.

I check back on Tomi. The comatose girl nods her head back and forth.

Calvin sets down his drink then branches off and looks at some art on the wall.

"Man," Floyd says, "y'all don't even know. A couple of months ago, we didn't have all this shit. Got this super rad VC to cosign. Some guy out of Menlo." He winks like I know who he's talking about. Probably someone my father knows.

"Get in on this shit now," Brennon says. "If we go big, that is. Sky's the limit."

Brennon can't sit still so he makes everyone a second round of drinks. Some dark liquor over rocks. He passes the drinks out to everyone except Tomi.

Floyd keeps talking. "This is like getting in at Google in the early days."

"She doesn't want one?" Jacqueline asks, pointing to Tomi.

"No," Charlotte says. "That's just Tomi, right?"

"Yeah, totally," Brennon says.

"So, what do you guys do?" I ask, looking into my drink.

"Oh, dude," Floyd says, clapping. "So glad you asked. You single, my man?"

"Kind of."

"That means you'll at least kind of like our website," Brennon says. "Take a seat."

Jacqueline and Calvin grab chairs. I sit next to Tomi. She doesn't seem to notice. Charlotte sits on my other side and crosses her legs.

Brennon stands in the center next to a glass coffee table. "So," he says.

"This is gonna be good," Floyd says.

"Yeah." Brennon gestures with his hands. "You may look at me now and not know this, but I used to be a total geek."

"*Hey, nerd boy,*" Floyd says, cupping his mouth.

"They used to call me that," Brennon says. "Then I got older. I realized I wasn't so bad, man. I just didn't have the confidence to try with any of the ladies. I was scared they wouldn't be DTF, you know?"

"Down to fuck," Floyd choruses in a rhythmic cadence.

Tomi nods in slow arcs. Her top catches sunlight from the long windows and shimmers like a disco ball.

Brennon speaks, pausing between each word, "*But if I had only known.*"

He lets silence hang for a moment.

"Known what?" Charlotte asks.

"Good question, young lady," Floyd says.

Brennon gestures. "If I had only known who was a prude or who was a slut, who had a secret horny streak." He rotates back and forth, catching eye contact with everyone. "I didn't know who was available and what they were looking for. So, I made a website where you can make a profile and find girls in your high school or college who may be into you."

"Not just for the fellas, either," Floyd says.

"Yeah," Brennon says. "All those girls, they really love attention. They can use the site to post whatever pictures they want. Guys can give them thumbs up or thumbs down. Get them to compete with each other. Who's the hottest bitch, you know?"

"Chicks love attention, right, Tomi?" Floyd says.

Jacqueline crinkles her forehead. Charlotte gulps her drink.

Tomi lets out a noise that might be a word.

"Think about it," Brennon says. "Like MySpace, except it gives the nerds a chance. I call it, 'From Geek to Elite.' That's who I'm doing it for, the geeks. Like you." He points to Calvin. "I bet you'd love to know which girls are looking for action."

"We're beta testing, now," Floyd says. "Every day, I log on. I see tons of hotties."

"Exactly." Brennon paces back and forth, a huge grin stretching his face. "Plus, you know, like, guys are picky, dude. All our parents, they didn't have this shit. So, they all broke up because they couldn't find someone with all the goods."

Floyd puts his arm around Tomi. "Like Tomi here. She could make a profile. She's like, 'Hey, guys, it's Tomi.'"

She sways with him, lurching like a puppet.

He continues, shifting into a fake female voice, "*I'm 21. I'm 5'4. I have tiny hands and feet. Brown eyes and black hair. I never have to shave my legs.*"

"Don't forget the measurements," Brennon says. "Big feature, dude."

"Tomi," Floyd says, "how could you let me forget?" He switches back to the girly voice: "*I'm a 32A with a 24-inch waist.*"

"Beautiful," Brennon says. "See, it's all based on logic. Just like coding, right, Floyd?"

"*Beep boop*," Floyd says, then laughs. "Coding robot at your service."

"He's the code monkey," Brennon says. "I'm the idea man. I'm like Steve. You know, Steve doesn't give a fuck. I love it."

"I can help you set up profiles," Floyd says to Jacqueline. He turns to Charlotte. "You'll love it. Maybe one of you dudes?"

"Don't forget the best part," Brennon says. He laughs, which sounds like a car backfiring.

"What's the best part?" Floyd asks.

"The real money maker," Brennon says. "All that data. There are people paying a fortune for it. I don't even know who. Their money is good, though; that's all that counts—the data."

"Okay," Calvin says, interrupting. He stares at his glass. The ice cubes have begun to melt. He sets it on the coffee table.

"I knew you'd want to use it," Floyd says, light golf applause.

"Wait," Calvin says.

Brennon and Floyd stare at him in anticipation.

"So let me get this straight." Calvin pinches the top of his nose. "It's like a dating site, except for underage girls, and you collect data on their bra sizes and save their pictures?"

Floyd turns towards Brennon. No one says a word.

Brennon's big grin deflates. "Why'd you say that like it's a negative?"

Jacqueline pulls her phone out and says, "Guys, I think, like Greg, just..."

"No," Brennon says in a shout. "Let him answer."

I activate SCAB. Floyd sits up straight, too. Charlotte sets her glass down.

"Don't you think," Calvin says, "that making a site like that is, I don't know, maybe a little gross?"

"I knew they wouldn't understand, man," Floyd says. "Everyone questions genius."

Brennon doesn't say anything, his eyes grow wider. Jacqueline starts typing something on her phone. "What floor is this?" she asks in a whisper.

"Fifteenth," Charlotte says. "Unit B."

Brennon's face darkens and he clenches his hands. Then he rushes out of the room.

"So much like Steve." Floyd shakes his head. "Temper and all."

"What just happened?" Charlotte asks.

"Hey," Floyd says, raising his hands in the air. "Don't look at me if he goes, like, full East Palo Alto on someone."

"So, it's been nice," Jacqueline says, standing.

Tomi rises, too, as if in imitation, eyes still glassy.

We all stare at Tomi. She opens her mouth as if to speak and then pitches forward onto the coffee table. Her collapse sends the glasses of rum spilling onto the carpet.

"No, Tomi," Floyd says, bolting up. "Not again."

Someone starts knocking at the door.

As if on cue, Brennon stomps back into the room, face twisted and tense. "Man," he shouts. "Those investors picked me. All our key stakeholders knew I'd have the best ROI!" He looks back and forth between Calvin and me.

I keep SCAB in full effect. The Celexa keeps my heart at a low hammer *thud* against my tensed muscles.

"Meathead," he says to me. "You even know what ROI means?"

Floyd tries to pry Tomi off of the coffee table. She bites her lower lip and a drool line of blood pools on the glass.

Jacqueline backs towards the door.

"Yo, calm down," Calvin says.

Brennon clenches and unclenches his hands over and over. Veins bulge along his arms and in his neck. "I drive a fucking spaceship," he screams. "It was people just like you in high school that told me I wouldn't make it." He gestures to his apartment. "This place."

"Five figs," Floyd says off-hand, dragging Tomi onto the sofa.

Tomi's arms dangle by her sides.

"Yeah!" Brennon says. "Look at me now. Who's laughing now?"

Jacqueline opens the front door.

Reiner stands there. "Ready to go?"

"Who the fuck is this?" Brennon says.

Calvin, Charlotte, and I follow Jacqueline to the door.

"Where are you fuckers going?" Brennon says. "I went to fucking Princeton. Charlotte, tell your brother we don't want him anyway. Fucking state school bitch."

"Woah, woah," Reiner says, putting a hand up. "Chill, dude." He turns to Jacqueline. "Who the fuck is he?"

Charlotte and Jacqueline step into the hall. Calvin and I follow.

Brennon comes to the door. "I said, 'Who the fuck are *you*?'" he screams at Reiner. His voice echoes in the hallway.

Reiner stands half a foot above Brennon, looking down.

Spit flecks fly from Brennon's mouth as he talks, peppering Reiner's Balmain knit.

"I'm going to need you to back the fuck up," Reiner says.

"Fuck you!" Brennon screams, making fists. "I could buy and sell your mom's neighborhood."

I barely see it happen. Calvin swings, his hand strikes out, fist colliding with Brennon's chin. The smack echoes against the sheetrock.

Brennon stumbles back into the entryway, looking dazed. The strike knocked a strand of saliva from his mouth, which hangs from his chin in a long rope.

Jacqueline laughs. "She leans into the doorway once more and screams, "No one gives a fuck about the Woz, you fat bitch!"

We sprint to the elevator.

Calvin presses his hand against the cold glass window. "Playing piano is gonna hurt for like a week," he says.

Going down, the ant city magnifies until nothing but the side of a building fills our vision. No brick—all flat, earthquake-proof architecture. We exit into a darkening evening.

Out by the building entrance, Greg stands next to Ken. Both smoke. Greg sees us coming and walks over like, "What did I miss?"

THE HORSE GIRL'S LAMENT

A taxi cab slides us into the Tenderloin. Rows of buildings line the street, rising up, offering a slit of the night sky. I would try to say something poetic like, "Venus rose in the great void, a pin-point of distant celestial light."

But how am I supposed to know?

The orange glowing smog swallows up the night.

Huddles of patrons dot the streetside before the Warfield's highlighter-bright marquee.

Yellow doors dump us upon cigarette-ash sidewalks. We huddle, like for warmth, in the UFO beam of a buzzing streetlight.

"That almost fucked our night up," Jacqueline says. "Why wasn't Sarah there? Was this your idea, Charlotte?"

Charlotte cups her elbows. "I'm not going to go into it. You can ask Sarah yourself."

Ken glances at the marquee, then at Jacqueline. "Didn't know you liked this sort of music," he says.

"When my dad lived in the Bay, we used to go to Gryphon in Palo Alto," she says. "He'd window-shop guitars. Said Joan Baez used to shop there. I got into acoustic stuff."

"It's cool," Greg says.

"People came from all over to play folk here," Jacqueline says, basking in the theater lights.

Inside the Warfield, framed posters tell a story. Photographs of concert crowds immortalized in black-and-white frozen euphoria.

Greg and Jacqueline start shoulder-tapping for beer.

Charlotte wanders away from us. She keeps her slim, salon-tanned arms tucked close to her sides. Reiner and Calvin start talking and post up by the double doors leading to the main auditorium. Charlotte disappears behind a wall of people. Calvin and Reiner lose themselves in a discussion, so I trace Charlotte's path through the buzzing crowd.

Using SCAB in tight places helps cut a trail.

Charlotte becomes visible, weaving up a set of stairs to the balcony. She clings to the handrail with peach nails.

When I track her down, she's on the second floor, leaning on the balcony, peering down at the gathering crowd.

She sees me approach. We stand together.

"You like this band?" I ask.

"Love them," she says. "I hope they play this one song. It's about horses: 'He Lays in the Reins.'" She puts her elbows together on the balcony rail. She makes a goblet from her palms and cups her chin. "You know that carnival in the summer?" she asks.

"Yeah."

"I went to the school nearby. I met Jacqueline and Sarah there. We used to be good friends. Then my mom made me a gymnastics girl. After that, I became a ballet girl. Then, last of all, a horse girl. My mom's the type to wear breeches to the grocery store."

"Weird."

"All over Portola Valley, you got these spots where you can get dirty and ride horses. Every tech wife has at least two horses. I used to go to this one ranch. My mom would stand in the middle of this sandy arena, shouting instructions to me while I rode. You get addicted to the smell of dust. Girls that ride for a while start to crave the scent of horse shit. So, I wanna hear that song about horses."

"For nostalgia about your mom?"

She laughs. "No, my mom is evil. I just like horses because they're really, really sad." She laughs again.

I slide closer to her and speak quietly as if someone is eavesdropping. "I don't think Jacqueline meant what she said about ruining the night."

"Of course she meant it." Her eyes meet mine. In the residual glow of the stage, she looks lost and scared.

That weakness makes me feel like I could almost fall in love with her. Either way, I get a bit hard.

"Sarah used to call the horse I rode, 'The World's Most Expensive Vibrator.'"

"That's funny."

"Jackie is being a poser. I was into this band way before her."

"I don't even really know them."

"You're into Sarah, right?"

"Yeah, like, maybe."

"Sarah and I had a little falling out after this awful party," she says. "But then she hooked me up with pills. If my younger self could see how cynical I've become..."

"My parents put me on pills when I was pretty young," I say. "Now, I can't tell you what it feels like to not be on pills."

She leaves me hanging for a moment.

The crowd sound barges into the silence between us.

"You probably want to know if Greg cheated on Jacqueline." Charlotte picks at her cuticles. "That fight at her party. You know what that was all about?"

"I thought, since no one talked about the fight, they resolved it."

"That doesn't mean the fight is over." She shakes her head. "You really don't understand women. Plus, it doesn't change whether or not Greg's dating someone else."

"Fine," I say. "Is he?"

She stares at the crowd. "Men can't help it. No one stops them, so they take what they want."

"You think all men cheat?"

She examines a hangnail. "There must be some guys that could stand a horse girl like me for a minute. I'm skinny. The guys call me petite and sweet. I'm there when guys want skinny women, and Jacqueline or Sarah are there for when guys want curvy women."

"I think," I say, picking each word, "that even though some men cheat, they can still love a woman."

"That's because no one treats you like an ice cream flavor," she says, shaking her head again. "That's what it is. I haven't met men who treat me like a lover, just like a flavor."

We stare at the crowd another minute before heading back.

Reiner and Calvin still stand guard by the doors. Greg and Jacqueline return with light beers in hand.

"Ready?" Reiner asks.

"Yes." Jacqueline smiles. "Let's go."

Greg smiles, too.

We enter the theater as the band takes the stage. Jacqueline and Greg hold hands. Something drops from their faces and slips between the cracks in the floor. I see the faces of Jacqueline and Greg as I knew them once, long ago in the land of sunny Polaroids. For a moment, they both look so beautiful that the mind comes up with all sorts of maudlin nonsense. I twist my head to the stage, and spotlights weave in patterns like fireflies. Then I'm back looking at Greg and Jacqueline. Some people look at beauty like that and think that hope exists. I look at beauty like that and hate the Brennons and the Floyds of the world even more.

Before the band plucks the first note, Jacqueline turns to us and says, "I wonder what the fuck was wrong with Tomi."

Then the band plays a song about horses.

OMENS

On the playground, we used to exchange stories.

Bring your craziest or your scariest stories. Maybe something weird happened to you. Maybe tell us something wild you overheard at school. You got an older brother who's seen some shit?

You'd hear boring shit like, "One time, a guy followed me for three blocks. He had this smile like an evil clown. Totally freaky, dude."

Or you'd read scary books from the library and repeat your favorite one.

I heard one that stuck with me.

The story goes like this.

A man walked into his backyard and looked out onto the field behind his house. There, in the middle of the knee-high grass, Death stood. The blades of grass around the trailing, black cloak drooped down into the dust.

With one skeletal hand, Death beckoned the man. So, the man began to beg. He asked Death to spare him. It wasn't fair.

Death listened and gave the man a series of tasks to perform.

Over the next year, the man performed each task that Death asked of him. He got his affairs in order. He reconciled disputes with everyone in his life. Became more successful than he'd ever been and discovered untold joys.

Each night, the man would revisit his memories—old and the new—and, in those glowing scenes of imagination, death seemed impossible.

At the end of the year, the man looked out to see Death standing in the field once more. When he approached Death, the man smiled, chest forward. He felt sure that he'd met Death's requests.

Death said that the man had completed all the tasks as requested. The man did quite well.

Then Death raised the wicked scythe.

The man began to scream and asked Death why he still needed to die. He'd done everything asked of him. He begged again, hot tears embracing his cheeks. All those memories he'd made. All he had done.

Death said that the additional year had been a generous offer. That the man had had the opportunity to accomplish so much. But that, now, it was time.

The man said he didn't care about accomplishing all those things.

Death asked what the man wanted if those accomplishments hadn't been enough.

The man said he wanted more time.

Death swung his scythe anyway.

The man fell face-first into the drooping stalks of grass, forever dead, which is, of course, all the time in the world.

After hearing that story, I became obsessed with death omens. Searching for the reaper's image everywhere. At night, I searched myself for lumps. I checked my pulse and felt the beat like a second hand against my index finger. I looked out my window at night, terrified that I'd see Death standing there.

At lunch, I would go to the edge of the field on campus. From there, I could see the kids sitting at tables. They played soccer and wall ball. The big kids in the upper grades looked like giants among us.

I'd stand against an oak tree. A big tree. Garbage-truck-big. The branches spread out, twisting like grandpa fingers.

That's where I saw him. Over-starched jean shorts. A bowl cut. Calvin, the kid in class who played air-piano over the desk.

We said, "Hey."

Then I said, "I heard this real scary story. Wanna hear it?"

My parents—nearing divorce—talked nonstop about bubbles bursting and market crashes. A decade of investment vanishing while startups ran amok. Home was a series of fights. But on weekends, one of my parents would take me to a nearby park.

Snaking train tracks, figure-eight, wound through the park grounds. You could ride a little choo-choo that seated eight. The engineer sat at the tiny engine, like a grown-up crammed into one of our school desks.

When the engine *chugga-chugg*ed down the track, my dad—who sat at the caboose—would sing this old blues song "Southbound Train." Picture this middle-aged tech businessman putting on a Mississippi warble and playing air-guitar in front of other families. But, you know, it might be what I liked about him the most.

In autumn, they did-up that park for Halloween. Black and orange streamers looped through tree boughs. Cobwebs caught kids on the jungle-gym like flies.

We travelled through the park, oohing and awing at everything. Me and my dad. This was after I got too old to hold his hand while walking.

We walked to the little train stop to take a ride around the park. There, I saw the reaper.

A clock tower overlooked the little covered train station and the reaper stood beneath the 6. Outstretched arms, secured with twine to the building. A black cloak billowing and cracking in the breeze. Plastic scythe clasped in bony fingers. Black and orange lights flashing in hollow eye-sockets.

Crowds passed back and forth beneath the tower, getting on and off the train, stopping at the snow cone stand nearby.

I tried to turn and head back to the cobwebs and the tree streamers.

My dad asked why I wouldn't go on the train. He thought I'd gotten too old for choo-choos. That day, he gave up and let me run back to where the other kids played.

For that month, I stayed on the playground, avoiding the train. I fought my craving for cola, wild cherry, and blue raspberry snow cones.

Then, on Halloween, my dad told me he wanted to ride the train. They had this night event. Families filled the park. Flashing lights, loud music, children in costume. He dragged me by my wrist to the tracks.

The reaper's eyes gleamed in the dark. We waited in line, and I kept looking up, watching the skeletal fingers for movement.

He managed to cram me onto the train, and we barreled into the night. My father looked back at the decorations. He pretended to tune his air-guitar. The train's wheels churned a steady rhythm, and he began to sing, "O, Death."

I watched the station fade from view behind us.

I don't really remember, but that might have been the last time I ever rode that train.

KEVIN'S SPEECH

What Kevin says, he says while standing on a picnic table in the skate park on one of those days day where we all have nothing to do but wait around. Kevin never really plans anything. If there is one thing about Kevin that you might find interesting, it's that he does stuff without a lot of forethought.

Today he wears heavy boots that you'd never want to take on a skateboard. Beneath his feet, you can see the many initials that people knifed into the table over the years. Jacqueline even scratched hers into the tabletop with a nail file.

Kevin lifts his hands in the air to add drama like a theater kid. He speaks.

"Given I've spent hours and hours on a leather couch, it's only fair. Only fair that my parents give one ounce of energy. Energy to sit on the couch themselves. Why aren't they there to sit beside me? They've put me on the leather couch because I don't have the stamina to endure the world that they created. The world that they've placed me in and got angry at me for not smiling."

I have a memory. My father took me to an electronics store one day. The one in Palo Alto. I was twelve at the time.

He drove the BMW, in which air conditioner blew in my face until my skin felt flushed and sick. He parked on El Camino and we stepped out onto hot pavement. My father wore khakis. My father wore a polo shirt with a little man on a little horse with a little hammer held above his head.

We went into the store and shopped for hours, walked over cool tiled floors, down narrow aisles. He wanted parts to build a computer. He said this PC he wanted to build could be more powerful than anyone's computer. He said he needed the right parts. Then he'd build it. Then he'd overclock it. Then once he overclocked it, he could do something with it. He'd need this computer to perform some unknown tasks for reasons I've never known.

In the store we'd see a thousand workers. Men in white button-up shirts, black slacks, red or blue or brown neckties. They had accents from Asia. My father said to me, "They all want my attention. They know all the parts I need. They'll kill each other for some of my commission."

I looked at the men with the accents. Some wore wire-framed glasses. Some had their thinning hair combed over to cover their shining scalps.

A man followed my father. My father told him, "You got lucky. You can help me build my computer." I remember the man. He was little more than five feet tall. His name tag read Gilbert, his skin two shades darker than my father. Gray hair sprouted in bunches from behind his ears. He smiled and nodded and pointed my father to motherboards. He led my father to hard drives, and RAM chips, and sound cards, and graphics cards, and processors. My father rambled to the man. He talked about the new BMW. He talked about his company's headquarters in Mountain View.

He talked about the garage with the model airplane where he first conceived of his company's ideas. He talked about a wise investor. He talked about building servers. He talked about his children's—that is mine and my older sister's—college funds. He talked of our tennis lessons and piano recitals and math classes outside of school. Meanwhile, Gilbert nodded and found power supplies and computer cases. He found one with a window in it, so that you could watch the computer fans whir. Whir like the propellers of a model airplane. Only now in this remote hour, I consider that, had my father the option to place a window in the side of my skull to watch what whirred within, he'd have written that check while my mother pushed me out.

So, I watch this. I'm standing on the tile floors that hurt my feet. I look down at Gilbert's shining dress shoes.

Then I look around. It's all dull gray. There are rows on rows of packages with arcs and neon colors meant to denote speed. Here I am watching one man talk to the other. They wear different clothes. But yet I'm supposed to accept that there is a difference in meaning between these two men. But all I see is the world's bitterness.

Bitterness is a hue of gray.

Gilbert goes to a back room to fetch some component for us. Then in a consummate moment, my father turns to me. My father lays out how he feels.

He says, "Don't ever end up like this guy working here. He has terrible English. He didn't go to college. He might be an illegal alien. He makes ten bucks an hour. He fights for commission. You'll never be like him."

Then when Gilbert returns, my father and Gilbert shake hands. I stood there, twelve years old, watching this happen. In this handshake I'm supposed to see meaning. I'm supposed to see why everything my father said makes sense. I'm supposed to see that there is such thing as all of this. For those who know my father, he believes that all the world falls into a clean and natural order. So, to signify this, he believes in tennis lessons and college degrees, little men on horseback with hammers. He sees the need for computers that move faster than all other computers. Computers that must be faster than all other computers for reasons I still have never known.

So, two years later, they catch me with marijuana. They catch me with coke after that. My father says he sees the type of people I hang with and tells me I'm not like them—at first, he does at least. But over time, he came to believe that I was of a different class of people, not Gilbert or my father and all was right.

But wait, let me tell you. One of the parts my father bought for that computer didn't work, and he rushed it back to the store because "some things are broken and you dispose of them."

THE DATE

*As a child, I lived in a quiet home. We all selected our words with precision.
Say too much and someone would jump on you, scratching your words apart.*

*Sarah tells me she lived in a silent home. No one said anything at all. When
she played* Gilmore Girls *and that opening song started, she felt like the sound
broke some ancient law. Like greasy burgers at a caviar party.*

A breeze blows Sarah's hair, and I catch her scent. She smells
like perfume, and I smell like cologne, and together we smell like a
fucking flower shoppe. She hugs me, and her breasts press against my
chest, and I think, *C, let's get to C, at least.* I activate the S, the C, and the
B of SCAB. That way, with my posture fixed, I stand much taller than
her, which I hope turns her on.

"You look beautiful tonight," I say.

Sarah's house sprawls out behind her. Jacqueline lost her mind
trying to figure out what kind of house Sarah had. It's just a big house.
Who cares? A little mismatched, with add-ons protruding from the
wings and two towering cypress trees flanking the property.

We walk around the side, through a latticed gate.

Sarah takes me down a set of flagstone steps. She drags the tail
of her emerald dress over the dusty steps behind her, and I want to
scream for some reason. In front of us, a lighted pool stretches across
most of the backyard.

On the opposite side of the pool sits a guesthouse. Amber lights
glow from the windows. A raised fire pit—made from matching tan
masonry—crackles, flames grasping up towards the evening sky.

Sarah takes my hand with her soft, moisturized palm. Her sleek
polished fingernails have the sticky feeling of a recent paint job. Her
heels click as we cross the patio.

Behind the guesthouse's French doors, a living room bathes in
golden light. Sofas sprawl in tan upholstery with lap blankets draped
over the corners. A glass coffee table and matching end tables shimmer.
Cream-colored curtains hang from dark brass rings. A popular Ciara
song, "Goodies," plays from a five-piece audio system.

Putting my hand into my pocket, I touch the side of my penis.
Still not hard.

Shit.

You'd think all the perfume, the song, the dinner would pump me up, but I guess not. When I first fucked around and kissed girls in junior high, the scent of perfume or fruit gum used to be enough.

Sarah turns to me and says, "You know, you look really tense. Why don't you sit down or something? Drink?"

An uncorked bottle of red wine stands beside polished crystal glasses.

She pours and carries me a glass. Then she sits next to me, the couch creaking. "I'm glad you made it." She lowers her voice.

"Thanks," I say because it's the only phrase that comes to mind. Everything else in my head says, *She's sitting next to you. Get to C.*

"Okay." She looks away. "Like, do you want dinner then?"

"Dinner sounds nice."

"Chefs prepared something special."

"I've never had anyone do this much for me. Why all the work?"

"I don't know," she says. "Thought you were super cute, so I wanted to spoil you."

This comment makes my cock twitch a bit. Not enough to start hardening but getting there.

"Jacqueline did say you'd be a bit shy."

We stand and bring our wine to the table. Sarah lifts the heat domes from each plate, revealing several platters of glistening entrees.

We fill our plates and settle in.

"I'm going to stick to salad tonight." She pulls some lettuce off her fork with her mouth. Her teeth make a terrible sound against the metal tines. She swallows. "I was a little nervous, still. Had to impress you."

"Oh," I say. My hand flicks at the side of my penis. From her angle, she can't see it. "I mean, I take some medicine for that. Anxiety, that is."

She laughs, "Love the honesty. I used to. What do you take?"

"Uh." I might be creeping toward C, but I can't tell. "I, uh, take Celexa."

Her eyes open wide. "I used to take that in sixth or seventh grade."

"Oh."

"Does it work?" She sets down her fork and leans forward. She places both elbows on the table and makes a shelf with her palms for her chin. Her propped arms press her breasts together and, even though she's looking right at me, I glance at her cleavage. Then I feel myself harden against my hand.

"Oh, yeah," I say. Then I smile big. "Like kinda."

"I'm glad," she says. "Sometimes you need the heavier stuff, though. Drink some of your wine. Loosen up."

"Like what?" I obey her orders, slugging half my glass.

"You know, the benzos. That's this big fancy word, benzodiazepine," she says.

"Jacqueline says she's been trying to find benzos." My penis now stands at C, and I flick it again to take it to B. I make sure to activate the B in SCAB. This makes me sit up more. "I think she's been feeling anxious or something," I finish.

"They aren't that bad," she says. "When you're feeling that big, terrible panic, they take it down a bit."

"I feel that feeling sometimes." The word "feel" tastes bitter in my mouth. The wine washes the flavor out.

"Worth considering. I'm just like you. I'm not like the most popular girl ever or anything. I get anxious, too."

"That's why I like you," I say. "I mean, that's why you're cool."

"Oh." She takes another sip of wine. "Want to watch a movie after dinner or something?"

"Sure."

We move to the couch when we're done with dinner. Sarah dims the lights. She puts a movie into her DVD player. Some sort of drama where I can't remember anyone's name. The protagonist has all these weepy voice-overs.

"I'm cold," Sarah says and pulls a blanket across our waists.

I stretch an arm around her, and her warm skin presses against me. I slide my other hand beneath the blanket and check the status of my erection. Without nurturing, I slid from B back to C.

Sarah presses her body closer to me and turns my head with her hand. Up close, her light-gold eye-makeup shimmers. She gives me a slow blink and places her fingertips against my chest.

When people touch me like that it sort of hurts. I take her hand in mine and guide it away from my chest, interlacing our fingers.

She presses her forehead to mine and lifts her chest.

This gets me going. A huge flood of relief. Her other hand rubs circles across my thigh, and I activate my leg muscles to impress her.

"I'm glad you could relax," she says, except the smell of Caesar salad dressing and garlic croutons hits me in the face.

"*Umm-hmm.*" I nod.

I pull her close and kiss her.

She moans and pushes forward against me.

Kissing doesn't help much because now I taste the garlic. My erection retreats towards B.

"You have any gum?" I ask.

She stops kissing me. "Sure."

My tension begins to ease while she searches the end table. She brings it back out and gives me a stick, then goes to put it away.

"You don't want any?" I ask.

"I thought you were the one who wanted some."

"I just guessed that you might also want some," I say. "Like, it tastes good." I put the stick in my mouth and chew away the remainder of the garlic taste.

She opens up the package and looks at the gum. "It's alright. Not my favorite flavor. I'd rather taste you." She leans against me.

I let her kiss me and consider sliding the gum into her mouth with my tongue. For my sake, the gum in my mouth creates a taste buffer.

The kissing intensifies, and Sarah moans again. "You know what?" she whispers. Her mouth is right up on my neck, and the heat of her breath turns me on.

"What?" I kiss her cheek.

"Even at the party, I thought about doing dirty things with you."

"Oh, that's nice of you to say." I'm trying to get my penis up to A. The Celexa fights back and my head swims.

"Yeah? How do you feel about that?" She grazes the top of my crotch with her hand. Her lips, wet with saliva, glide towards my neck, and she—

"I think I need to go to the bathroom," I say and stand up.

She looks at me. "Okay?"

"I'll be quick."

Inside the bathroom, I pull down my pants.

"Fucking B," I whisper. Then I start tapping myself against the cold marble countertop. I turn the sink on and run my hands under the water. I look up into the mirror.

After rubbing and stroking some more, a hot, sweaty feeling starts on my back.

"Fucking Celexa."

"You okay?" Sarah asks from outside.

"Yeah." My voice echoes on the bathroom tiles.

"Come back." Sarah knocks on the door.

The sound makes my cock twitch once.

I look at the mirror again. "Fuck it."

I slip myself back into my pants and exit the bathroom.

When I walk into the living room, SCAB activated, Sarah says, "Oh wow, someone's happy."

"What?" I ask.

I forgot to button my pants or finish buckling my belt.

"Sorry," I say.

"Don't be sorry." She takes my wrists. "Sit down."

I obey like a good boy. The way she orders me around gets me going, bringing me back to B, again. "Do you want to fuck?" I'm eager to get it over with while I have a bit of a hard-on.

She's looking at her feet. "Do you like my toenails?" She crinkles her bare toes. "School colors."

"They're nice, but..."

She sits down next to me and kisses me, pulling at my lips with her teeth. She presses one of my palms against her breast and I brush against where her hard nipple sticks up.

I picture my shirt coming off and her look of disappointment at seeing my body. This makes me activate SCAB.

She pauses a moment and looks at me.

I'm not touching my cock, but it feels like a B, still.

"Take off your shirt." Something about her voice makes me think of Jacqueline.

I almost swoon. Without hesitation, I pull off my shirt.

I flex my chest, shoulders, arms, and stomach. She looks over my body and the pain of contraction mounts. I squeeze my fists so that my arms bulge even more. With held breath, I wait.

Then she leans over to kiss me, which causes me to exhale the stale air into her face. She pulls back a moment.

I kiss her so she stops looking at me like that.

She pulls down her top and shows me the goods. Then she pulls my pants down.

I keep SCAB activated.

She strips my underwear right off and, to my relief, I'm standing straight up.

She sighs and, for a second, the medicinal fog breaks. A hot wave passes across my skin. My muscles come to life, and I'm about to lose myself to momentary passion.

That's when her fucking phone rings. The sound jolts me and my cock starts a painful jerking.

"Sorry." She answers the phone. "What? Charlotte?"

The fucking bitch ruining my night with Sarah.

Sarah mouths, *Sorry*, again. "No, Char. Stop. You need to chill on the fucking pills. You'll fucking kill yourself with that shit."

Charlotte's thin voice stings through the earpiece.

"I'm kind of busy." Sarah speaks in a loud, slow voice sort of like the signals is bad.

I start to deflate, losing sensation.

"Just chill out," Sarah says. "I'll call you back in a bit."

She shuts her phone.

"Charlotte bugged me for Vicodin but can't handle it."

I play with myself, shaking back and forth. A strand of pre-cum drips from the end and lays in my public hair like a thread of spiderweb.

"Poor thing," she says.

I begin to jerk on myself.

"Stop touching yourself," she says. "I will."

I keep stroking, trying to get things going again. Everything stays at C.

"Stop." The commanding voice returns. "I'll have to spank you if you don't."

That catches my attention. The warm relief floods me and my blood starts pumping.

"Allow me." She gets on her knees, bending over my lap. Her tongue flicks back and forth against my head. Her teeth almost hurt as they brush the shaft.

I squeeze my fists to keep my forearms full. I pound my fists against the couch cushions as she works. The blowjob goes on and on. Then this creeping lack of sensation starts in my cock, and my mind wanders off. The Celexa haze arrives, clouding up my mind.

I want to scream out loud, *Stay at A!*

Sarah works harder, her mouth moving up and down. Faster.

The sudden terrible image of returning to C and drooping causes the hot sweating to start.

"Here." I pull out of Sarah's mouth. I start masturbating, using Sarah's spit as a lubricant.

She sits there on her knees, and her eyes lose focus.

I feel too soft. The skin has this coldness to it that freaks me out. So, I stroke myself harder.

Sarah looks up at me, and our eyes meet. "You want me to suck it, again?"

"In a second."

Images flicker across my mind. All the nastiest porn I've ever watched. The first *Playboy* I jerked it to. Greg stole that one from a drugstore. Miss April, reclining on a sofa. Those were the days a still image could make me cum. But nowadays, it's women tying each other up with rope. It's forced orgasms.

My cock still feels cold. So, I dive into every thought I've ever deprived myself of. A sequence of flesh-colored images slips through my mind. I play out every sexual fantasy I can in the space of seconds. Then my cock starts to pulse again.

"Almost ready," I say. But I can't stop working my penis.

I think about Sarah doing things I'm too afraid to ask her to do. I think about J—

"Okay, put me in your mouth," I say.

Sarah does, and I cum right away, my load jetting against the roof of her mouth.

She drools and spits it on the ground. She puts a cupped hand out to catch any of the cum-spit from snail-trailing the front of that pretty green dress.

"You could have warned me," she says.

While climaxing, I activated SCAB so hard that now my hamstrings start to cramp. I give her a stiff smile.

She goes to the sink in the adjoining bathroom to wash the cum out of her mouth. I massage the backs of my legs because it feels like someone's stabbing me. But then I look at the angle of my biceps when I rub my legs. Extending my arms makes my muscles look small, and Sarah will be back in a moment. So, I lean into the couch cushions and position my arms so that they look good. Unable to massage my cramps out, I sit there and suffer.

She comes back from the bathroom and sits down next to me.

"That was fun," I say.

"I ran out of mouthwash," she says.

We watch the rest of the movie, and then we kiss until it's time for me to go.

ARRANGEMENT

Sarah says that if I do a couple things for her, she will suck me off whenever I want it. But first, she says that she sees how I tap my hands—which is a sign of anxiety (so she says)—and that I need some help. She says that doctors can amp up the dosage. I tell her I'm maxed out on Celexa. She tells me they can "add an olive to the drug cocktail," or some shit. That olive, she says, could really help me out.

She says the next time I go to the doctor, I should ask for Klonopin—which I do—and my doctor will give it to me—which she does.

The Klonopin kind of puts you out for a while. You can take a nice long nap. You wake up and can't remember shit. If you smoke weed, you really can't remember anything.

"I don't like it," I tell Sarah. "Makes me too tired to work out. I feel weak."

Sarah sits on the sofa in her guesthouse. A lap blanket drapes her legs. She shrugs and says, "That's okay. Not for everyone. You gave it a shot, though."

The open windows invite cool air.

"Yeah."

"How's your sex drive today?" she asks.

"Bad. I think the Klonopin made it worse."

"Lame," she says. "Maybe you should stop taking it then. You want all the extra dick-sucking to feel good, right?"

"Of course."

We sit there for a while and make out.

Then she says she has an idea. "Don't throw the pills away. I could flip them. I already have the connections."

"I guess." I pull out the pills and go to hand them to her.

"You don't want me to pay you for them?"

"No," I say. "Oh yeah, you said you would give me blowjobs for doing something, but I forgot what it was."

"Oh, that," she says. "Well, I'll get to that. But first, how about you give me the pills then. That can be the first thing you do for me."

She takes the pills out of my hand and giggles a little.

After stashing them away, she kisses me for a while.

Sarah—she tells me that her business goes up when kids quit their anti-depressants. Sometimes, they cut the meds on their own. Sometimes, their doctors think they've had enough. Sometimes, things change, or they get into the right school. The drugs gripped their serotonin production and, without the meds, it takes ages to regain their natural production. So, these kids search out means to boost what their brains suffer to create. That, or numb out the pain of withdrawals. They wind up on a new drug that way.

"Your parents ever put you on meds?"

"No." She shakes her head.

The pool party last summer thrashed the house. She thought that would be it. Her parents would unleash new rules and restrictions. But what scared her was how mad her father didn't get.

"Sarah," I say. "You got off easy. My dad used to get pissed at me for needing to count all my actions seven times."

She laughs. "My dad got back and started talking about what colleges he could get me into." Sarah kisses me. We've kissed long enough that it's becoming a sort of routine, nothing new to be expected.

"I want to fuck you," I say.

"You do?"

"Yeah." I try to quicken my breathing to show her I'm telling the truth.

"I've got something for you to do first."

"What's that?"

"Before that," she says, talking about the task—not the sex.

"What?"

"Tell me what scares you the most."

I tell her the rats in her garage can pass her rabies or the Hantavirus. That rusty nails through skin might mean punching your clenched teeth out to sip your food. The wrong can of vegetables might mean death from botulinum toxin—the same nerve paralyzer that you can inject into your forehead and cheeks. I tell Sarah that castor beans can produce deadly ricin or be part of a balanced meal. Doing push-ups in a dirty bathroom can expose you to all sorts of germs.

"Why would you do that?"

"Never mind."

She tells me that those were a lot of ways to die but not much to be afraid of. "I know what's in your head," she says. "The same things my dad fears."

I tell her that I'm nothing at all like her dad.

Her eyes meet mine and her pupils contract in examination. "Terrified of losing control," she says.

Somewhere nearby, we hear the Amtrak blare. I don't know whether I should shake my head or disagree with her.

She says she has to be careful giving opioids to kids on certain anti-depressants. That people can die from serotonin poisoning. She says she didn't mean to start selling drugs to people. She just didn't want to take what her parents gave her and that was a decent way of disposing of them.

I interrupt, "What did you need of me again?"

The sun has begun to set, leaving the living room in the half-light. Nearing the time one flips on lamps.

"Follow me," she says.

VILE

"I'm going to Sarah Lawrence," Sarah tells me. "My father set up an appointment with the Dean of Admissions. So, do something for me when I'm gone." She takes me past the threshold, down the single dark hallway that runs through the guesthouse. A bedroom opens at the end. Lampshades and upholstered chairs—the color of over-chewed bubblegum—adorn the space. "Better than what I gave Greg," she says. "A real bitch to get it."

The air in the room dries the eyes.

Sarah digs a narrow, glass tube from a dresser drawer. "This 8-ball goes to Kevin. Way better than the crap he sells."

Parallel lines of light, slicing through the blinds, reveal the vial.

"If you lose it..." she says. She doesn't finish the sentence. She hands me the vial. "I want this out of here." She looks around like someone's watching.

"I get it," I say.

"You don't get it. My brother got the shit and made some weird, spacey girl deliver it. The girl that gave it to me, she stuck it up her pussy so that she didn't get found out. Went to the ER with an infection. Four days at the hospital!"

"Up her pussy?" I ask.

"Yeah."

I lift the vial to smell.

"Why?" She puts up a hand.

I laugh, but she doesn't. The coke disappears into my jacket.

"Glad to see it go."

"I'll miss you when you go to Sarah Lawrence. I'm glad you're applying to Stanford, too." I reach out to hug her.

She backs away. "Just get it to Kevin," she says.

"What do I get out of it?"

"Blowjobs." She smiles, but her eyes stay on the spot in my pocket. "Don't you remember? I told you that already."

"Have time for one now? I think my sex drive..."

She looks at me and shakes her head. "Don't tell anyone you got this from me. I'll fucking stab you if you do."

Jacqueline arrives in her gold Lexus. Sarah walks to the car and bends close to the driver's window. I stand some ways away. The scene reminds me of my parents after the divorce.

The cold wind plays with a cypress tree.

Jacqueline sticks her head out of the driver window to air-kiss Sarah on the cheek. Her eyes catch the sun and look like electric-blue lights.

The Lexus flies freeway-fast in an after-hours school zone. No kids to splat on the asphalt. Jacqueline cranks a Rob Zombie song to sledgehammer-volume. Rob croons about his Dragula.

"Don't get us stopped," I say.

"I'll let them look down my shirt." She smiles.

I check out her V-neck Hollister sweater. My hands sweat, fingers wrapped around the skin-warm vial of coke.

Menlo Park remains cop-free, and we stop at a grocery store in the Heights. The Lexus lights spotlight a picnic table out front.

Skinny Greg and skeletal Charlotte chill at the tables. Jacqueline grabs the knob and deafens us. The speakers beat my ears to pulp. Greg and Charlotte turn to face the car.

We slide out of the sedan and over to picnic tables.

"What are you two doing here?" Jacqueline asks. "Thought you were alone," she says to Greg.

"Same." Greg points his thumb at me.

They suspend a tense silence. My cock gets a little bit hard. Like warm-candle hard.

Charlotte shrieks and gives Jacqueline a gentle hug. "Sorry," Charlotte says. "I haven't peed in like two days."

"Why?" I think of Elmer's and Super Glue, and then I sweat.

"Vikes," she says. "But I squirted a few drops in the bathroom just now."

"Some asshole kicked her out for taking too long," Greg says. Across Greg's chest, a skull on a white field. A cockroach crawls from an empty socket. The Drug Bugs in a dripping Halloween typeface. Around the collar of his shirt, white saliva residue sticks to the fabric.

Charlotte glistens with sweat. She shifts from foot to foot. "You think a rubber tube would work?" Charlotte asks.

"Get a turkey baster," Jacqueline says, turning away.

Charlotte glances back at the store.

"Don't prolapse your pussy." Greg laughs.

"I'm going to try the bathroom again." Charlotte dances towards the automatic doors.

"Make sure she doesn't die," Jacqueline tells Greg.

He scuttles after Charlotte, shoulders slumped, not practicing SCAB.

"The bitch is gonna pop like a water balloon," I say.

"Good." Jacqueline keeps her arms in a tight X across her chest.

Some starchy private school types pass by.

"I'm going to call Calvin while we wait," I say.

When Calvin arrives, Greg and Charlotte make their return.

"Maybe a thimble," Charlotte says.

We cram into the Lexus. The water balloon squeezes between Calvin and me in the back. Jacqueline takes the long way out of the parking lot, going over every speed bump she can.

Cool air rushes into the cabin as Greg cracks a window to blow smoke. "You look beautiful today, babe," he says.

Jacqueline drives with her right hand. Her left hand cradles her head, elbow propped on the windowsill.

"Totally hot," Greg says and inhales, hissing smoke through his teeth.

Charlotte groans.

At the park, a bed of fallen leaves blankets the grass. The moon, ghost-white and full, lights up the sky, merging with city lights and blocking out the stars.

Ken and Jasmine stand in silhouette beside a cement table. We approach them.

"Freezing," Jacqueline says, cupping her elbows in her palms, arms crossing her chest.

I offer her my jacket.

She thanks me. But it should be me thanking her. Without a jacket, my arms look more impressive.

Charlotte trails behind us like a toddler, cradling her distended bladder.

"She's trying to pee," Jacqueline says to Jasmine.

Charlotte makes a crying sound. "She's still trying to get her father's attention."

Jacqueline turns around, glaring. She looks pretty hot in my jacket.

"What are we trying to do?" Ken asks.

"I need wine or weed or something," Jacqueline says. She reaches into her bag and pulls out a bottle of Mad Dog 20/20.

"You saved the day, Jasmine."

Charlotte lies on the top of the cement table, staring at the sky. Ken and Greg break off and talk while the rest of us drink Mad Dog.

Jasmine lights a clove cigarette and pages through a book she brought with her. "You, you, and you," Jasmine says, pointing to Jacqueline, Calvin, and me in turn. "All of you have moons in Cancer." She lifts her hands, palms exalting the moon, smoke snaking through the crisp air. "The full moon tonight is also in Cancer."

Jacqueline shakes her head. "Are you a matchmaker or something?"

"Like, no," Jasmine says, sucking her clove. "Kinda spooky, right?"

"What?"

"That the universe brought us all together."

"No."

Charlotte cries and rolls back and forth. "I'm dying."

"I'll go check on her," Jacqueline says.

"Cancer moons take care of everyone," Jasmine says.

"Oh, please." Jacqueline walks to Charlotte and rakes a sweat-damp clump of hair from the poor girl's forehead.

A rush of night air puckers my arms.

"So, what are you thinking?" Jasmine asks Calvin.

"Dude," he says to me. "I don't know if I ever told you this. You know the back of your house? You used to run up to the fence and twist at an angle so that you could see my back window."

"Yeah," I say, "so I could wave when we wanted to play video games after our parents fell asleep."

He nods.

Jasmine puts her book away and focuses on Calvin.

He says, "Here's a story and, after that, maybe you won't think about the window the same. Anyway, I took lessons with a teacher in San Francisco. She taught at a studio in Chinatown, a few blocks from where my uncle lives. My uncle, he used to take me to lessons. He'd buy me sesame buns on the way home. My teacher, she had these rosy carpets and a beautiful metronome over the piano. She would sit in an armchair overlooking Stockton Street. This was the year she taught me Beethoven's 'Piano Trio in D Major.' We played the song several times in largo. Me, working the sustain pedal. Her, gazing out the window. When I finished, she said something that surprised me. She said, 'I never liked the metronome.' I didn't know what she meant. Seemed weird, right? But she said that she could feel something off about it. Like when she used it, it brought some sort of bad luck. You know, stuff old people get freaked about."

"Like, why?" Jasmine asks.

Calvin nods. "Her grandfather bought the metronome. This was during the Chinese Exclusion Act years. He didn't have a piano in their tiny place, so he'd put the metronome on and play ghost piano to old songs stuck in his head. She never knew him because his apartment fell in during the 1906 earthquake. He was a young man. My teacher's mother was out at school at the time. The only thing they pulled from the rubble was the metronome. She became obsessed with that metronome. Thought she could hear the earth rumbling when she played. But she kept it anyway. I asked her why. She said that she needed to. That if she had to face it and use it every day of her life, then it wouldn't affect her so much."

"Did it work?" Jasmine asks.

"I don't know. She said it still freaked her out." Calvin looks off through the trees. "But I guess we all need music in our lives. It's there for us. Anyway, I went home after one of my lessons. I walked into my bedroom. That's when I saw this guy standing there. He stared out the window at the hills in the distance. A young dude who looked a bit like me."

"Freaky," Jasmine says.

"At first, yeah. I got that cold feeling. It shot right through me. He didn't move. I called out. No response. As soon as I stepped towards him to check out who he was, he disappeared like an illusion. He popped out of existence. Left no trace behind."

"What the fuck?" I ask. "You never told me that."

"Messed me up a little," Calvin says.

"Like you saw a ghost?" Jasmine leans forward.

"I don't sleep well," Calvin says. "You all know that. Been real bad lately. I watch for him on some nights. Got my blanket up to my chin. I'll open my eyes every once in a while, to check."

"Have you ever seen him?" Jacqueline asks.

"A few times," Calvin says. "Maybe on nights with a bright moon like tonight. I can tell he's there because the room gets cold. It can be the middle of a heatwave but, when he's there, the temperature drops. I crack my eyelids and see him there, near the foot of my bed, staring out the window. I try to catch a glimpse. Maybe ghosts are the memories that a place keeps."

Charlotte's groaning interrupts us. She sits up, hands splayed on the stone slab of the table. "I'm really fucking dying," she screams. "I don't know. Maybe, like, take me to the hospital. Fuck."

"You'll be fine," Jacqueline says and shivers and stuffs her hands into the pockets of my jacket. Her facial expression shifts, and she looks at me.

Before she can act, Charlotte shouts, "You're one to talk, Jackie. Your boyfriend does whatever he wants—if you know what I mean."

"What do you mean?"

"You're butt-hurt that Daddy doesn't give you any money. You're too hot for burnouts, but you just don't have the look to be a popular type. Just Jackie—the nobody."

Jacqueline takes her hands out of the jacket and balls her fists.

"Fuck off, Jackie. You don't have shit. You want to be a doctor or something, but I guess failure is more fashionable. You just can't get over the fact that your dad sucks and your mom gave up after he left."

I shuffle toward Jacqueline, focusing on the pocket with the vial in it.

"Fuck you, you anorexic slut," Jacqueline says, leaning over Charlotte.

"Yeah, yeah," Charlotte says. "I've heard it before. Go back to wasting your life."

Jacqueline lunges at Charlotte and grabs the skinny girl by her shoulders. She shoves Charlotte back on the tabletop.

Charlotte lets out a weak yelp.

I become apple-hard.

Jacqueline gets on top of Charlotte, pinning her wrists to the tabletop.

I adjust my cock as I inch closer to the fight. With one hand, I reach out and slip it into the jacket pocket.

Jacqueline unleashes a series of insults at Charlotte.

My hand finds the glass vial.

Then Charlotte moans like she's having the world's greatest orgasm.

Jacqueline and I look down at the same moment. Just in time to see the urine jetting from the opening in Charlotte's skirt.

Jacqueline jerks back, and I yank the coke out of her pocket.

We all stand there, watching a torrent of strong-smelling piss as it floods the table.

Charlotte laughs and laughs.

When I get home, I empty the vial into an empty creatine container. I put the glass vial into my sock drawer.

BLUE RASPBERRY

Jacqueline tried to blind me. When the curtains went up, she bleached my whole room. My forehead cramped in response. So, I had to share the pain. We went to Calvin's house. Since he was still sleeping, we blinded him, too. Made his whole world go bright white.

Jacqueline noticed a patch of coarse skin on my arm. She asked since when had I started skin-picking. I told her she knew since when.

The pavement melted chewing gum. Jacqueline pulled a tube of something from her purse. The lotion she spread across my arm felt warmer than my skin. She rubbed it in like she was trying to actually heal me or something. I thought I'd melt against the burning asphalt like so much ice cream.

She handed me three horse pills. Gabapentin. She said I needed something sweet. Calvin took one, too.

There was a field, but it wasn't a field. Sometimes it was a fairground. And when it was a fairground, great wheels turned.

In daylight, you couldn't have seen the many golf ball bulbs. They garlanded everything and waited for the night.

Greg and Ken joined us. We bought blue raspberry snow cones.

Greg asked, "What the hell is a blue raspberry?"

Calvin looked down at his melting cone and said, "A thing that doesn't exist but keeps trying."

Greg laughed, but I didn't.

Jacqueline said the cold hurt her teeth. She said it didn't taste much like raspberry.

Something made my muscles feel light.

We all four crammed into a cart that took us up into the blue summer sky. Going up, it felt like my chest grew with every heartbeat. On the way down, that stomach full of funnel cake and cotton candy and snow cone lost all its weight.

We spun around until we sprawled across a patch of grass. Jacqueline took another Gabapentin. She said it made everything sweet.

Four dads took to the stage at the center of the fair. They played old songs from their time. I told Calvin how great it'd be if we were on stage, playing songs from our time.

I told Jacqueline that she was right about the Gabapentin pills.

She told me the effects sort of fizzle out if you take it too often.

After dark, we walked through crowds.

You stop smelling the funnel cakes after a while, even if they're still there.

The beam from a stage light swung out into the crowd. It passed over Jacqueline's eyes and electrified them. When I shut my eyes, her blues floated in the dark. So, I kept my eyes closed for a while.

Calvin asked if I wanted to ride the Ferris wheel with him.

There was a fairground. But sometimes, when you looked at it from above, it was a box of jewels.

Calvin held another blue raspberry snow cone. He said, after some time, it just tasted like sugar.

I said at least it tasted sweet.

He said too bad it wasn't real. Too bad because, he said, as a child, it didn't taste like sugar. It tasted like blue raspberries.

Crews of workers started to shut down the rides.

The fryers—where the funnel cakes were made—cooled off.

From our spot on the grass, only one ride shined in the dark. The golf balls glowed cobalt. It looked like some mythical hedge where blue raspberries grew.

Then someone shut the ride off, and it was like they blinded us.

DOSE

Sarah grinds a cigarette into ash and tells me about Dose. She says she met him after getting her license and a car. Dose sat on a bench near the muddy banks of Lake Lagunita. This was at a time of year when the lake had some water in it. Her brother introduced them. On the bench sat her brother, a female friend, and Dose.

She asked why everyone called him Dose. But her brother said Dose studied business administration. What Sarah noticed about Dose were his cyclist legs and rock-climber arms, the five o'clock shadow on an angular chin. The female friend sat in the middle of the two men. She wrapped a knit cardigan over her chest, her beautiful lonesome eyes cast out at the lake.

Dose and Sarah took a walk around the lake. He asked her what she liked, and she said her psychology class. She said she enjoyed problem-solving. Dose liked recursion. The idea that you could make a program loop forever. Somewhere in that exchange, they traded numbers.

Sarah loves a specific shade of blue. The hue resembles swimming pools on a summer day. When her insides go from pacing to screaming, she can sit on a chaise by her pool. She can watch the shadows cast by ripples that crawl across the bottom.

Just before poolside season, she invited Dose over. She gestured to the backyard, pointing to a spot where a band could perform: a stretch where a bar could stand, an enclave for sitting and socializing.

She said he looked at her with the eyes from a Vermeer painting.

He wrapped a wiry arm around her. He took her inside.

She said the first sex with him felt careful. That's what she said, careful.

They had sex in the same careful way for a while. Then Dose asked Sarah to star in a fantasy.

She would sit on the sofa in the guesthouse. She'd leave the doors open because it was the season for open windows.

The curtains moved in the breeze. They looked the way seagull wings look, the way the birds seem to float up in the air.

He let her have a drink on the table and a cigarette burning.

Then Dose would walk up—this was the plan—he would walk up, and they would start a conversation the way strangers do.

At some point, he would make a move on her.

She needed to fight. He said she could fight hard.

She hit him with the insides of her wrists. She squirmed back and forth, just playing around.

But then he grabbed her throat and drove her into the cushions. She said it's true what they say. Rock climbers have strong grips.

He tried to pull his belt out in a single yank. The way they do it in the movies, with a whip sound-effect added. But he couldn't get the belt out. He stood over her. His penis poked between a spread zipper, looking like dangling meat over a shark's mouth. He kept trying to get the belt out.

She almost laughed, and she told me later she was glad she didn't.

He got the belt out and stuck his penis into her. After a few pumps, he wrapped the belt around her neck and ratcheted it up. Then she started clawing and leaving red drag marks across bands of lean muscle. Behind her, the seagull curtains rose and fell.

He said at some point she needed to play possum. To stop struggling. To go limp.

She asked if he'd prefer that she keep her eyes open or closed.

He said he'd let her choose.

Because of the breeze, she went with eyes closed.

So that's what she did. She let her arms drop on the couch beside her. Let her head lull to the side.

Dose kept pounding until he pulled out. The belt remained tight around her neck. Bolts of light shooting in the dark.

When he was done, Dose sat on the couch, staring up at the ceiling.

She asked him why everyone called him Dose. He said it wasn't that interesting. The year he moved to off-campus housing, he dropped acid a couple times with Sarah's brother. He said he fussed over the dosage so much that people called him Dose. He said he didn't—doesn't—want to lose control. Not even for a second. Sarah told him that was very interesting. He said acid is such an underclassman drug.

Sarah lost count of the number of times she performed in his fantasy. I'll let you pick a number in your head.

But the last time they fucked, it was a day that would have been perfect for a pool party.

That time he tightened the belt so hard that Sarah lost consciousness.

She woke up with a scaly crust on her stomach. A note lay next to her on the tan couch cushions. It said that Dose had to go to the lab. But he checked to make sure she was still breathing before he left.

She sent him a text message and asked him to stop seeing her. He said it was okay.

Then she set her phone down and had to go out onto the patio and look at the pool for some time.

I ask her if she is afraid that he will come back and kill her. Not in a pretend way.

She says she doubts he will come back. After all, he seemed to crave, above all else, her utter erasure. Maybe distance would provide that.

I tell her I don't quite know what she means.

She says she's just glad that he never came inside her.

"I'm sorry," I say. "Do you want me to fight him or something?"

Sarah plays with her lighter, flicking it on and letting the wind whip it out.

I tense up so that maybe she'll look at me like I'm strong. There's a part of me that really does want to fight him. I already don't like this guy because of what he did to Sarah but not in the way you might think. I don't like the guy because he got to be intimate with her in a way I've never been.

Across the pool in the main house, all the lights turn on at once.

I must have startled, because Sarah laughs and coughs from the smoke.

"That's the security system. It flips the lights on at the same time every night It's my favorite time."

"Where are your parents?"

She stares at the upstairs windows where warm light slices through the blinds. "Sometimes I look for a really long time and I think I see someone there just waiting for me to come home, but I don't want to come home because I don't want to know for sure that no one's there, so it's better just to sit here and dream."

Somewhere in a tree, a bird makes a sound, and I'm back in my room as a child with the window open, and there's no pain, just me on my bed in the mauve light of summer evenings with that bird and its melancholy voice in a nearby tree and my parents together in the room next to mine.

Sarah coughs.

I clear my throat. "I guess at least you have your own TV in the guesthouse."

But as I was saying, after Sarah and Dose split, she spent a lot of days staring at ripple shadows. Then she looked to the spot where a band could perform. An area where people could socialize and a place to put a bar together. So, she went online and started inviting her friends to a pool party.

NO SURPRISES

We see it coming. This time it surprises no one.

A few of us enter the skatepark. Just an overcast Thursday with wind raking across our faces and the last of the leaves falling.

Greg tosses his backpack against one of the fences.

Somewhere nearby, we hear a single shriek, maybe the tape girl.

"Bitch," Greg says to no one in particular.

Jacqueline stares through the chain-link fence at the passing cars. The road backs up, all our classmates honking and blaring music.

Across the park, Charlotte emerges, her little hands twisted like a ball of yarn. She walks towards us with a sense of purpose that feels a little creepy. Just Charlotte cutting across the park, across the apocalyptic landscape with something resembling inevitability.

She stops, looks up at Greg, then glances down at her little ballerina shoes. But when she picks her head up again, her mouth curls up like a smile.

"You hear what happened?"

Jacqueline, Calvin, and I stand together, faces like, "No, what?"

I watch the way Jacqueline examines Charlotte and, for a moment, I'm struck with a realization as to why Jacqueline's been so hostile to Charlotte. Something in Jacqueline's eyes resembles loss, but the news of the day doesn't allow me time to sit with this recognition because Charlotte continues to speak.

She says, "Kevin took the last train out of the mid-town station yesterday morning."

"What do you mean?" Calvin asks.

"Like he's gone, dude," Charlotte says. "Train squished him."

"Damn," Jacqueline says. She looks at me.

"I guess he kept telling us he was gonna do it," I say. "Well, not outright, but sometimes you can feel it."

Calvin keeps his hands dug deep into his hoodie.

Throughout the park, we see everyone huddled in groups, and the energy of the place hums like flies on piles of beached kelp. If you were to walk into this land of dried-up pools, you'd think that something exciting had happened, but Greg, Jacqueline, Calvin, and I just continue to stand, something heavy dropping inside our stomachs and anchoring our guts down with it—a feeling like freefall—and no one ever teaches you what to do at times like this, not ever.

So, to you, if you stood in the backyard of your suburban home, and you heard us—the chatter from the park, the words from our kind of person—you might think of those sounds the way you'd think of a dog barking on some distant neighbor's patio: nothing but a failed communication.

We go over to the drugstore and barge in. The store glimmers in red and green. Some sickening music leaks from the speakers. We ask around, hunting down Kevin's old co-workers. They all say the same shit, that he quit a week back, and that the last time they saw him, he seemed super happy—too happy.

When the last of Kevin's co-workers head back to work, I turn my head just enough to see Calvin pick a large marker off an end cap and slip it into his pocket.

Back at the skatepark, Reiner joins us. Still, no one skates. Everyone leaves their boards along the fence. "When did it happen?"

"A little after rush hour," Jacqueline says. "Probably just hobos on the train at that time of day."

"He was kind of a dick," Reiner says. "I'm not surprised."

Some kids sit around like a little cult and sing Radiohead's "Karma Police" together. When a new group of people arrives at the park, everyone races to tell them. Calvin and I stay behind.

"Kevin used to play double bass in the orchestra," Calvin says. "Sat by the piano. We used to talk. This was right before hormones fucked us all up."

"I remember that Kevin," I say.

"Why do you say *that* Kevin?" he asks. "Same dude."

"Feels like he wasn't the same." I shrug.

"Do you even care?"

"Kevin used to joke about suicide all the time."

"But, like..."

"I'm just saying that it isn't surprising," I say.

"This one time," Calvin says, "Kevin convinced us that a ghost lived in one of the bathroom stalls. This was back when the school walls all had D.A.R.E. posters leftover from the fucking Regan years."

"I remember," I say. "Spike Lee and Harrison Ford and Nicolas Cage telling us to READ."

"Yeah," Calvin says. "You were there. That time we gathered a bunch of bouncy balls and footballs and hurled them over the stall wall, screaming, trying to drive the ghost out."

"Yeah."

"Kevin really wanted to get it," he says. "He kept screaming, 'I see it! I see it!' Wanted to stay in the bathroom past the last lunch bell."

Jacqueline listens to our conversations. "We are all gonna see ghosts," she says. "She points to the tracks. People started calling it Suicide Alley, especially that stretch along Alma. I hate crossing the tracks. How can no one feel their presence?"

Jasmine arrives and draws a bundle of sage from her backpack. She dances around the park, leaving smoke trails behind her like a sky-writer.

We watch her sway like we're trying to read what she's writing.

Everyone keeps to the edges of the park.

When the late afternoon drives the sun towards the horizon, dragging it towards the distant foothills, Calvin gets up and heads towards the bathroom.

I follow behind him.

He finds a patch of untouched tile. The sick, greenish light from the buzzing fluorescents casts moon-pools of reflection on the grimy porcelain.

Calvin uncaps the marker and squeaks it across the wall.

There is something about this act that I can't watch, so I turn away, the act of confession too much of a burden. I leave Calvin in peace.

In Las Vegas, on the Day of Armageddon—when the gamblers crawl from the casinos, blinking into a new sort of wasteland—they won't act surprised; they're used to disappointment.

But surprise and grief aren't exclusive terms.

Overnight, the phrase "**Kevin was here**" appears across town. A vain fight against erasure. Slot machines beside an atomic bomb.

On the Day of Armageddon, we all die. No matter how many push-ups you can do, the same fate awaits us all. But we do one more like it'll be the deciding vote.

I alter my routine and perform four movements per muscle group. I begin a creatine load after a short reset.

I return to the gym and down a flask of creatine and protein. I attack the weights with endless reps until my arms get light and shaky.

A warm feeling builds on my neck. It spreads down my back the way a fever does. The sort of feeling when you don't want to drag yourself out of bed. No matter how many curls I complete, the sensation grows worse. I do another and another, trying to kill this feeling.

The skatepark starts to resume its regular rhythms. Boomboxes blast and croak. Skateboards roll back into the dried-up pool husks.

On the Day of Armageddon—if any of us survive—we'll find a way to do it all over again. Hurdle right back towards a glossy Apocalypse.

TRIBUTE

At Kevin's high school, they hold a funeral for him. The flyer reminds me of *American Idol* in two ways. According to the schedule, the event spans about one episode in length, and there are numerous threats of atrocious singing.

Some bitch takes the stage and starts belting the most ear-bleeding cover. One of those awful songs with too much warbling.

"That cunt, like, didn't even know Kevin," Jacqueline says. She sits next to me, wearing a black dress.

On my other side, Calvin keeps his hands buried in sweater pockets. "I think that's his sister," Calvin says.

"Oh." Jacqueline squints as if to verify this. "What the fuck?!"

After the singer finishes, she smiles and walks to the corner of the stage, balancing in her high heels.

A blotchy-faced woman that we're told is Kevin's mom starts hugging the girl and petting her shoulders. Everyone golf-claps.

I get up and head to the bathroom. Reiner comes with me. We both piss then stand in front of the mirror together. He locks the door.

"Got any coke?" he asks.

"I don't do that shit," I say. "Plus, I gave what I had to Kevin. Before, you know."

"Shit," he says. "I don't have any hash." He starts digging around his breast pocket. "Klonopin?" he asks. He pulls out a baggy with a couple small pills in it.

"I thought the bottles I give to Sarah are like the only ones around."

He shrugs. "I find shit."

"Sure," I say and take the pill.

"Dissolve it under your tongue, or you won't get the full effect before we gotta leave."

The pill tastes terrible.

Kevin's dad takes the podium. He looks like the sort of fuck who you'd beat the shit out of in grade school.

"Kevin never asked for help," the fuck says. "Such a strong will. I know that more than anyone."

No one laughs.

He licks his lips.

A hot pulse starts in my head, and I switch into SCAB.

"Kevin should have come to us a thousand times," he says. "It's a hard world, an unfair world. The kind of world that takes hard work. That can scare people. They want out of it."

The pulse pounds harder, like a drummer coming to kick my ass. The microphone that awful bitch sang into looks like a hammer. A hammer to smash this fucker's face a thousand times with while the audience sits and listens to the *thunk*s and feedback squeals through the speaker. That image produces an incredible feeling until the Klonopin hits.

Watery waves pass through facial bone. My left ear rings for the duration of his following sentence.

"So, if we learn anything from Kevin's death, it's that, maybe, you should ask for something like help. Make sense?" He nods and then leaves the stage. Then the singing bitch sashays back on like some nightmare Vaudeville performer to fight her way through "Greatest Love of All."

When she finishes struggling, Greg and Ken take the stage. This third guy wheels out a drum kit. They make us all sit while they set up. My head feels droopy, but I continue to watch.

"Alright," Greg says, then looks down at his feet. "We have a song that's, like, dedicated to Kevin. I mean, not about him, right? But, like, maybe about some of the feelings he had."

Jacqueline balls up a Kleenex on her lap. Then she begins ripping strips off it.

The drummer counts them in and then goes into a savage D-beat. Greg and Ken enter with a pounding bass and guitar attack.

"Stupid motherfuckers, shut the fuck up!" Greg shrieks into the microphone.

Reiner laughs.

"All I fucking wanted was a moment to myself,
All you've ever wanted was to put me on a shelf.
Every single moment brings me closer to defeat,
I try to feel anything, but nothing left tastes sweet."

Greg thrashes from one end of the stage to the other while Ken plays a manic guitar solo. Each note feels like a pleasurable piece of broken glass shoved right into the side of my face.

The singing bitch stands to the side, laughing with one of her friends.

Jacqueline's tissue lies in ribbons.

Greg rips at the bass strings like an archer trying to knock an arrow. The drummer starts blasting. He loses and recaptures his cadence, speeding toward an utter loss of control. A sprinter running downhill.

The Klonopin swells in my chest. My arms go lax and my face tingles.

Greg sings, "*Spit my blood in your eyes. What's the reason to abide?*"

When I check on Calvin, a few tears roll down one of his cheeks.

Ken loses his guitar pick and starts grating his knuckles against the strings. Greg's hands look like two steel rakes, attacking the frets and strings. Then Greg's voice switches into something soft. A thin, ringing note floating over the crushed-gravel guitars. A single phrase repeated again and again.

"*...And I can't slow down.*"

Right as the Klonopin surges in my blood, I look to the stage and see Greg and Ken, their faces twisted into something earnest, and it strikes me that, if I were the one on stage playing, I would feel naked, and I would do anything I could to cover my nakedness. I look to the stage, and a thought passes through my mind that, up until this moment, has never even occurred to me. I think, *Are we just stupid kids?*

Then the Klonopin overtakes my body, and it's all just white noise.

Candles from the dollar store tap against each other inside a plastic bag. The bag swings from the crook of Lore's elbow. She bends over and begins placing them in a semicircle—plucking them from the bag one at a time.

She crouches down and works while the rest of the service guests exit the auditorium.

I say, "I'm sorry. It fucking sucks."

She puts a framed photograph against the tan wall.

Kevin wears a leather jacket, no expression, Lore at his arm. An undecorated frame boxes the picture in.

She doesn't look up. "It was the coke. He got a bag from someone."

"Oh."

"The day he died, I left him at my place while I went to the corner market for cigarettes. All the coke made him a real dick."

In front of the frame, Lore places a couple of toy Tech Deck mini-skateboards.

"Heading back, I see all these cars lined up. A stopped train. That mechanical arm blocked the track. The bells clanged, giving me a fucking headache." Lore pulls a lighter from the plastic bag.

The breeze makes the flame flicker back and forth. She flicks again and again to keep it lit.

"People scream and crowd around. Something trapped between the wheels."

"Gross," I say.

"You know?" She glares at me. "You remember when we all had braces?"

"Yeah."

"Picture someone ate the shit out of a big, bleeding steak." She gnashing her teeth. "Then they go to smile for a family photo with all those chunks of meat gumming up their braces."

"Hated when people let that happen."

"Yeah," she says. "The wheels of the train looked like that. Braces with chunks of food in them."

"Gross."

"Totally. You never need to see what it looks like when a train hits someone." She shakes her head. "He laid down on the track, they tell me. I bet if he stood up, it would have just flung him, you know?"

"You think the coke did it? For real?" I rub at the back of my burning neck.

"Yes, for real," she says. She reaches into the plastic bag again and pulls out a 40oz of Miller Light. "He loved this," she says.

"Loved it?"

"Yes, I love it, too." Then she laughs. "I loves it," she says in a girly voice. She laughs again.

"Did you snort the rest of the coke or something?"

"Couldn't," she says. "Cops took it."

"No way."

"What the fuck do you think happens? You a cokehead or something?"

"No."

"Damn it," she says. "I was hoping you had coke." She unscrews the cap and begins dumping it right onto the concrete in front of the shrine. Clusters of foam bubble on the ground. Some of the people filing out turn and look at her.

The liquid splashes. Several large droplets spatter the photograph. Ink bleeds, and watery circles form on the image.

She turns to face the people filing out.

"Lore."

"What?"

"Nothing."

"He loved you all." She crosses her arms over her narrow chest. "All you guys at the skatepark. You should know that. Every night, when he got back, he'd say, 'Remember what Ken did?' Something like that. Laughed like a big kid."

"I mean..." I shift from one foot to the other.

"Yeah," she says. "I'm going to miss Kevin, too." She screams at the people leaving the auditorium: "Fuck most of you!" Then she spikes the empty bottle onto the ground.

The glass shatters and skitters across the concrete walkway.

She walks away, boots clicking. The flames flicker in the wind.

On my way home from the service, I stop at the pharmacy and refill my Klonopin. When I get home, I take two tablets, letting them dissolve under my tongue. A taste like licking wet cement.

THEY NEVER PREPARE YOU FOR ANYTHING LIKE THIS

The body trains itself to respond to whatever the mind anticipates. Kevin once said you can guide yourself through a skate bowl, balanced between body and memory.

But Kevin can't guide me now. That's the thing.

The sound of the breeze sends me leaping out of my skin. A creak from the house settling becomes the pigs banging down the door. Here to arrest me for my part in Kevin's death.

The body can't sustain it forever, though. The furnace inside my chest burns out and offers a sick-ward calm while it prepares to heat once more.

Every morning, after I take my creatine and Celexa, the panic takes swings at my chest. Then I pace a groove into the carpet.

Sarah calls me, and I head to her house. She tries to massage the tetanus tension from my shoulders, but her hands feel like intruders.

I jerk away from her the way you do when your hot shower goes cold all of a sudden. She tries to fondle my cock out of my pants to the same effect.

She watches me with something like pity or regret. Then she tells me I should probably go if I don't want to hold her.

I walk from Sarah's place down to the pharmacy. There, I ask for a refill of the Klonopin. They believe me when I say that someone stole my other bottle. What I don't tell them—of course—is that I emptied the last bottle in less than a week. They call my doctor and get the pills ready. Once outside, I place two of them beneath my tongue.

At the spot where Kevin died, you wouldn't notice a thing out of place. Like someone erased Kevin from existence.

I scramble around in the gravel—scraping up my kneecaps—looking for anything; searching for a lost tooth or a busted-out filling; scanning for bone fragments or bloodstains; holding my breath like that will help.

Nothing.

You'd think someone would usher me away from the tracks, but no one seems to notice.

When I give up, a slick sweat covers my back.

I take another pill to blunt the feelings.

Back when I invented SCAB, I used to beat bruises into my legs and arms. Every day, on the bus ride home, I'd slam my thighs with my fists. I'd angle blows at my shoulders and neck. If I could withstand my own relentless beating, then no one could hurt me. I'd get numb to the pain. Let their wildest haymakers bounce off me. I'd learn to endure anything and everything.

Once, I beat my legs so hard that I had to limp home from the bus stop. I called it progress. Whenever anyone asked about it, I just told them I had a big leg day.

You could take all the beatings in the world, but they never prepare you for anything like this.

Calvin sinks into an armchair inside the old bookstore. Beside him, an indoor plant takes in the beams from a skylight. Through the glass, the sky reflects a dull gray. I take up a spot on another chair.

"Remember when we used to have sleepovers," I say. "We'd sit cross-legged on the carpet and talk all night. The sun would rise, and we'd be tired, but, as always, felt a little bit wiser."

He says, "I feel so trapped."

But I talk over him in rapid-fire. All the crap about Kevin spills out.

He sighs and sets his book down. He says, "You'll have to figure out whether or not you can live with it."

"I don't know if I can deal with it forever."

"Our conscious existence," he says, "is nothing but a collection of things we tolerate living with."

Never take the nights that you can sleep for granted. My sheets plaster to my skin. Through a slit in the blinds, I watch the street.

I try to scratch the thoughts out of my head, rolling off the bed and pressing my face against the carpet.

A dizzying vision of the train tracks materializes. A spot where I lie and await the blaring train. The earth will shake and rumble like a California earthquake. An unbearable, overwhelming sound screeches above me.

Then nothing remains.

I imagine the moment it hits me and shreds every inch of gym-grown muscle.

I bolt up and take another Klonopin.

When I next see Sarah, she's sitting on a chaise lounge by the pool. Through her sheer wrap, I can see the curves of her body. In the endless snow of Klonopin, a warm image appears. I picture myself kneeling on the gritty pool patio and kissing Sarah, begging for her love. But then the image fades back to nothing, the same gray Celexa numbness sucks it away.

"I missed you," she says in a flat voice.

We kiss.

"You look sick." She looks me up and down. "I know you took Kevin's death hard but, you know, maybe you should chill a little."

"I'm not that sad. That's the thing, it isn't sadness."

"Good," she says. "I need something from you."

"Yeah?"

"Any way you could get a refill on your Klonopin?" She combs through her beautiful hair with her fingers. "Just tell the pharmacist that someone stole it."

"No," I say, "I tried."

"I thought you didn't like it?"

"I don't, but I know you do."

"That's sweet of you," she says in that flat voice, again. "When you can get a refill, let me know. I got someone who's buying a lot of it. Call my cell. I'll be out of town, remember."

"I'll tell you as soon as I can."

Sarah leaves to go to a fundraiser dinner in Palo Alto.

Once I've walked a few houses away, I retrieve the bottle of Klonopin from my backpack and take two.

can Fly

In science class, we chop up pigs. Our teacher pulls them out, one at a time, from a red-and-white sports cooler. We pair up with whoever's next to us. That puts me and Calvin across the table from Greg and Jacqueline. We all look down at our pickled piglets. Shriveled, pale lumps, eyes plastered shut.

"Looks like a graveyard for cops in here," I say.

Greg laughs.

The room stinks with a sick chemical smell. A smell like dying alone in an old folk's home.

"It's your chance to practice for med school," Greg says to Jacqueline.

She doesn't say anything, looking at her pig.

"I could stick a rod up its ass and make it a puppet," Calvin says.

"Why?" Jacqueline asks.

I try to open our piglet's eyes. The eyelids seem to stick closed. "So, we start with incisions, up near the shoulders," I say. "Make sure to cut wide."

"Sorry, Babe," Jacqueline says to the pig, and then she slips her scalpel into its hide. "Then down the chest."

It takes more effort to slice through the thick of the chest.

"Don't cut so deep through the stomach," Jacqueline says. "That's what the instructions say."

My scalpel makes a smooth slit through the abdomen.

"Made your final cut?" Jacqueline asks. "Make it look like a big X."

"Yup," Calvin says, looking at my work.

"Now we peel it back," I say.

The skin fans out like a flasher opening a trench coat. Tiny organs inside, shining like beads. Calvin pins the flesh flaps down to the corkboard beneath the pig.

Greg does the same.

"Maybe they'll let me trepan you next," Jacqueline says.

Greg crinkles his forehead, confused.

Jaqueline smiles. "It means drilling a hole in your head. Then I'll see all your secrets."

Greg looks away then puts out his hand for the scalpel. "My turn," he says. "By the way, Jacqueline, you didn't cut high on the chest."

"Whatever," Jacqueline says as she hands him the scalpel.

Greg starts hacking away at the dead pig's guts.

"Stop," Jacqueline says. "Do you want us to fail?"

Calvin shakes his head. He looks at me. "Wanna pin the lungs?"

I say, "If they didn't die now, they'd grow up, get nice and fat. Then someone would chop them up for bacon."

"Stomach next," Calvin says.

I slide a pin into the thing. The pale gray tissue dimples, then allows the pin in.

"Hey, Calvin, I'll give you a buck to eat its heart," Greg says.

"Nah, dude."

"We're supposed to be pinning the organs, idiot," Jacqueline says. "Find its liver."

Greg picks up a pin. "Oh, it's here," he says. "Wow, this dead pig liver is healthier than yours, Jacqueline."

Jacqueline shakes her head.

"You okay?" Calvin asks Jacqueline.

She flushes pink. "Not feeling great."

Greg looks over at her and then starts swirling the guts with a pin.

Jacqueline looks down at the black stone lab table.

"Your fault for fucking with hard shit," Greg says.

"Did you really fuck someone else?" Jacqueline asks him.

Calvin looks down at the instructions.

"You been taking those pills still?" Greg asks.

"Shut up." She shakes her head, hair hanging over her face.

"Suck my dick, Jacqueline," he says.

She looks up at him. "Did you fuck someone else?"

"I'll give you back the shit that you left at my house," Greg says.

Around us, groups of students work with notice. They pin organs and peel flesh.

"You piece of shit," Jacqueline says.

Greg shrugs. He turns to look at the instructions.

Jacqueline reaches with both hands to grab the pinned-down pig.

"The fuck?" Greg says, turning back.

Jacqueline tugs on the pig. The skin flaps pull back, further skinning the pig as she pulls.

"Woah," Greg says and repeats the phrase a few more times.

She drags the pig off the table and lifts it into the air. The guts tumble out of the opening and hang like a flesh mobile.

Other students watch this unfold. Some laugh.

Jacqueline throws the pig at Greg.

It *thunks* him in the chest, dumping the rest of the guts onto him. It falls onto the floor with a *slap*.

Before the teacher can say anything, Jacqueline turns and stomps out the door.

We all stand there a moment, in a haze of formaldehyde fumes.

Imperial Jade

"You're all spread out like teenagers," I say to everyone when I return from the restroom.

They sprawl across two booths. Behind them, the scenery speeds by like a video cassette on fast-forward. In one booth: Greg, Charlotte, Ken, and Jasmine. In the other: Jacqueline, Calvin, Reiner, and me—once I've taken my seat.

Calvin rubs at his elbows.

Jacqueline looks out the window.

"The fuck is going on with you and Greg?" I ask her.

"Don't ask," she says. "Don't mention the pig either."

Greg turns as if he overheard his name. "You good, babe?"

"Yeah. Headache."

The train stops at the San Mateo station, and people exit.

Charlotte applies a layer of lip gloss and puckers at her reflection in the window. Ken pulls a flask from his bag and passes it around. We all drink some kind of strong dark liquor until the flask empties.

Jacqueline grabs my shirtsleeve.

I flex—a reflex.

She gets close enough for me to smell the cloying alcohol on her hot breath.

The sick heat of it makes me want to kiss her until the whole train and everyone on it vanishes around us. Actors on stage until the lights go out.

"I bet Sarah finds some college guy on her trip." She laughs so loud, it hurts, throwing her head back.

Everyone turns to watch.

"I think Sarah's going to choose Stanford." I can't bring myself to push her off me.

"What do you mean?"

"Like that she's gonna stay in the Bay Area."

Jacqueline clears her throat. "Hey, did she not tell you? No way is she going to Stanford."

"Come on." I shake my head.

Jacqueline shrugs. She reaches into her purse and rummages for a minute. Then she pulls her hand out and palms a pill into her mouth. "For the headache."

Calvin looks out the window at the dashes of rain striking against it. "Good to see San Francisco in its natural state," he says.

We exit at the San Francisco platform and divvy into cabs that resemble our booth arrangements. Rain splats on the sunroof. The cabby plays talk radio at a low volume. We don't say anything during the drive.

The cabby leaves us in front of a shop on Stockton Street. Through the glass facade of the storefront, we can see our other friends shuffling inside.

We follow them indoors. A security guy eyes us from his post by the door.

Greg and Charlotte gawk at a display case. Unseen lights illuminate rows of jade pendants and rings.

"Look at that one," Charlotte says.

On the other side of the counter, a woman my mom's age watches them.

Jacqueline walks to another case.

Calvin and I follow her.

"I've wanted a simple gold chain forever," Jacqueline says. "Keep meaning to buy one. I guess I was hoping one would, you know, come to me." She looks over the case. "These don't cost anything, either."

"Do you need more jewelry?" I ask.

She turns to me. "You're fucking ridiculous."

Charlotte's voice whirs overhead like a violin. "I love that one."

The woman behind the counter slides the tray of jewelry out and places it atop the glass display case.

"Can I?"

The woman nods.

Charlotte chooses a deep green pendant from the velvet tray.

The woman behind the counter looks Charlotte over. "Imperial Jade," she says. "For health."

"I want it so bad." Charlotte holds it to her throat and postures in front of a little mirror.

"Maybe he can buy it for you," the woman says, gesturing to Greg.

Greg lifts his chest up.

"He better not," Jacqueline says.

The security guard by the door turns to us again.

"Come on," Greg says. "What do you even want?"

"Don't do this," I say to Jacqueline. I take her elbow.

Jacqueline can't speak. She wavers on her feet.

Reiner moves to stand behind Greg and break the line of sight. "He won't buy it," I say.

She turns and pushes through the door, ringing the little bell. I follow her outside.

"It's ridiculous," she says. "He acts like I'm not there."

"You don't have to do this," I say. "Why keep going?"

"I want it to work."

"You can't embarrass us like that."

She exhales and puffs her cheeks. "I'll keep it together. But, I mean, what the fuck?"

We wait outside long enough to see the day darken. Wind rushes up and over the hilly city, cutting through our clothing. Then the bell rings, and everyone pours onto the pavement.

Greg walks over to Jacqueline and kisses her cheek. "It'll be okay," he says.

"We have dinner plans down the street," Reiner says. "Let's go."

Our group starts to shuffle along the pavement.

Calvin waits behind. He stares across the street to a window just above the line of shops. He seems to lose himself in a trance then returns to us and follows down the pavement.

Inside the restaurant, a woman leads us to a booth in the back. Two benches run parallel on either side of a shining blond-wood table. We order tea and seal ourselves inside with a sliding door.

Jacqueline and Greg sit side-by-side for the first time all night.

Steaming tea arrives and we pour ourselves cups.

Ken and Greg talk about video games, so Jacqueline turns to Calvin and me.

"I remembered something," Jacqueline says. "Calvin, you mentioned seeing a ghost after visiting your teacher here."

"Yeah," Calvin says.

"Any new sightings?"

Calvin cradles his head in his hands for a moment. "Sorry, head hurts. Yeah, I mean, I'll explain."

The green tea revives some pleasant feelings in me.

"If you go looking for ghosts, you won't find them," he says. "I learned that. You expect them, you don't find them. But sometimes you get lucky. They'll reveal themselves when they're ready."

"Like, did you think he wanted something?" Jacqueline says.

"I told you I see him sometimes. Sometimes the temperature drops and I only feel him. One night, the temperature shot down and I peeked over the top of my blankets. He stood there in his usual place. Always standing there. Then I started thinking that it wasn't what he did or wanted. We expect to hand a ghost a coin, an old doll, a family photo, and they'll vanish, having been satisfied. But that's not right. I realized it was what was inside him that mattered."

"He has ghosts of his own," Jacqueline says.

"Yes." Calvin nods and rubs at his eye with the sleeve of his shirt. "He was trying to find out what haunted him. I was so concerned with myself, my pain, my ghosts, that I couldn't see the same thing in others, even when it was right in front of me."

We order our food, and Reiner announces, "I'm going to a private school next year. Not that any of you will miss me."

Calvin leans to me. "I thought I could sleep over winter break," he tells me. "But those two weeks, I couldn't sleep well. It's like all that stress changed me so that, even when the stress isn't there, my body still acts the same."

"Fucking sucks," I say.

Food arrives and conversations blur between us.

"I'm having trouble peeing, again."

"My dad never bought me a new car."

"I can study for my SATs way better with coke."

"They'll make me wear a fucking uniform there. How fucking East-Coast-embarrassing."

"That's where Sarah's at."

"We know."

When Charlotte leans forward to grasp at a bottle of soy sauce, Jacqueline breaks off mid-sentence. Everyone else quiets.

From Charlotte's scrawny neck, the jade pendant swings back and forth.

"Please don't tell me you bought that for her."

"Jacqueline, come on," Greg says.

"No," she shouts.

"Jacqueline," Charlotte says.

"I don't want to hear it." Jacqueline slaps her palms against the table. All the little cups of tea rattle at once.

"You treated me like fucking shit," Charlotte says.

"You *are* fucking shit," Jacqueline says. "Don't have any real problems, so you make up a problem by starving yourself."

"That's too much, Jacqueline," Reiner says.

"It's hard for me." Charlotte's face looks like it did on the balcony at the Warfield.

"Real hard being rich," Jacqueline says.

"At least I am rich," Charlotte says. She leans over the table, letting the bangle dangle from her neck. "Your mom still lives off of a divorce. Your dad doesn't buy you cars or take you on college trips. Just a fucking cliché Menlo Park mom."

"Fuck you." Jacqueline gasps like I do when I'm having a panic attack. "I'm leaving," she screams. She tries to crawl over Calvin and across my lap.

"Jacqueline," Calvin says, "I'll let you out. Give me a second."

But Jacqueline's shoving her way through the booth. She elbows me in the eye and throws the sliding door open.

Calvin and I follow her. Everyone else stays.

On the curb, Jacqueline stands in the rain. "I have to go," she says, panting. "Please, don't stop me."

"I'm sorry," Calvin says to her.

"I'm done with him," she says. "It's over. He's not even brave enough to come outside and get broken up with. Doesn't fight for the fucking relationship, either."

We listen to the rain for a while.

HOTEL

We trudge towards a hotel in the Mission District. To a place that Jacqueline reserved with very different room arrangements in mind.

Greg takes Charlotte into his room. Jacqueline takes the other room. Ken and Reiner follow Greg, while Calvin and I follow Jacqueline.

She pulls open the mini-fridge and takes out handfuls of bottles. She snaps them open and swallows them.

Calvin sits at the end of one of the two queen-size beds. I find an old-fashioned wing-back chair beside the dark, draping curtains.

The hotel room boasts an old San Francisco charm. Mirrors that look like the windows on a ship, they hang beneath gold lights. Through the opening in the curtains, San Francisco twinkles in the night.

"Don't overdo it," I say to Jacqueline.

"Shut up." She sits on the carpet and leans against the bed. "We've dated all of high school."

Calvin lies back on the bed, staring up at the ceiling.

"Throw me a tequila," he says to Jacqueline.

She tosses him one of the small, gold bottles.

"I thought you two wouldn't make it past the whole pig thing," I say.

"I really didn't want it to end."

"Why?"

Calvin sips the tequila.

"I don't know." She tries to open a bottle of vodka but then tosses it aside. She goes on, "All those fucking people that call love a verb. It isn't a verb, it's a noun: routine—or maybe habit is the right noun. The action in a noun like routine is implied, making it passive, weak."

I say, "He got scared that you'd be the only person he'd fuck for the rest of his life."

"I'm starting to believe that," Jacqueline says.

"Hand me tequila," I say. "I'll have what he's having."

"Only got silver."

"Any limes?"

"No."

We each consume a bottle.

"Why wouldn't Greg be happy with just me?" She tosses an empty bottle at the waste basket and misses.

"I guess guys see other women and start wondering if they're missing out," I say.

She laughs, "He could have picked much prettier girls than Charlotte. You feel that way about Sarah or something?"

"I don't know."

"You know," Jacqueline says.

Calvin sits up and looks at a painting on the wall.

"Sex isn't that great, if you're asking," I say.

"Is it true what they say about chubby girls giving the best head?"

"Whatever, give me a whiskey."

"Maybe you should slow down."

Calvin says, "I'm single, but I guess I don't have much to look forward to."

"Why is that?" I ask Calvin. "You're better than all of us combined."

"Chill out, who are you? Nick Carraway?" Jacqueline says and laughs.

Calvin laughs.

Someone knocks at the door.

"Fuck," Jacqueline says. "I'm not getting it."

I stand and walk to answer the door. Through the peephole, Reiner's face stretches out in the lens.

When I pull the door open, he says, "Greg wants to talk to Jacqueline."

"No way," she says, still sitting against the bed.

"Probably not a good idea." I start to close the door.

"It's between the two of them."

"Here." I step into the hallway and shut the door behind me. "What is it really?"

"He's worried about her," Reiner says, crossing his arms.

"I don't believe that."

"No." He shakes his head. "He says she started getting hooked on something. He's worried about her."

"But he fucked around with Charlotte," I say.

"They never hooked up. They kissed a few times. He went to her for comfort."

"You're just listening to his side. They definitely hooked up."

"You're taking her side," he says. "What's the difference?"

"Even if all he did was kiss her, that's bad enough. Plus, he's a cokehead."

"I'm not saying he's perfect. But pills? Much worse than coke."

"No."

"He wants to talk to her. He's in there crying. Just persuade her to talk for a minute. Why are you white-knighting for Jacqueline all of a sudden?"

"I'll think about it."

Back inside, Jacqueline looks up at me. "What was that about?"

"Nothing," I say. "Not worth your time."

We fall asleep for a few hours. When I wake, rain patters the window. There's something special about waking in a city on a rainy night. Like a peace with the ugliness of the world or some shit like that. Jacqueline sprawls on one queen mattress, Calvin on the other, curled up and facing the wall.

A knock at the door. Must be a repetition of the knock that woke me.

Through the peephole, Greg stands in the hall.

I swing the door open and slide into the hall. "The fuck do you want?"

"That's my fucking girlfriend in there," he says, sour alcohol on his breath. "I'll talk to her if I want to."

"No, dude," I say. "I think that's over."

"Stop trying to protect her. She's not so much better than me. Neither are you, you fucking..." He trails off and steadies against the wall.

"Go back to fucking Charlotte," I say.

"She isn't great," he says.

"Why play around with her then?"

"I don't know." He shakes his head. For the first time all night, his face reads of genuine pain. The pain isn't for Jacqueline, but for his own lack of control. "Jacqueline matters to me," he says. "I don't know what's going on with my life. I miss you too, dude." He looks up, face darkened with weeping.

The sight of him makes me activate SCAB.

I leave Greg in the hallway.

Inside, Jacqueline sits upright in bed. "What the fuck did he want?"

"More of the same."

"I want to go home."

Calvin, who up to this point has appeared sleeping, speaks, "Same."

We head downstairs and take a cab towards the train station.

San Francisco persists through the darkest hours of the night. Dawn is still hours away.

A second cab follows us into the parking lot for the train station. We race towards the train as it slides to a stop beside the platform.

Greg gets out of the second cab, waving his hands.

Calvin and I get on the train, and Jacqueline waits on the platform for another moment, considering Greg. Then she turns away from him as if to say, *Goodbye.*

The train jets away from the station. Greg stands alone beneath the dull orange overhead light, shrinking then disappearing.

The train draws out of the bright city lights along a sleeping part of the peninsula.

Calvin reaches into one of his pockets. "Jacqueline," he says.

"Yeah?" she asks, facing him.

"I got this for you," he says.

He draws out a simple gold chain.

TO BECOME NOTHING AT ALL

When my father recreated his life in a new home, he included nothing of my mother's. The gifts and photographs and trinkets never made it to the new place. He left the whole relationship at my mother's house.

Sarah tells me that her parents still aren't divorced, but they really should be. She says that her mother has objects—has things. That anywhere in the house you go, you'll run into something belonging to her mother but it still doesn't feel like her mother lives *there. She adds the emphasis to the word, "Lives," leaning forward while she does it.*

I kiss Sarah. I missed her while she was visiting Sarah Lawrence. Our tongues grate against one another. We squeeze our lips together. I pull her close to me, but the sensations stop there. We break apart, leaving a small spider silk of saliva hanging between us.

"Charlotte still has to recover from whatever the fuck happened in the city," Sarah says. "I'm going over to see her. Girl stuff."

When I leave Sarah's house, I dwell over Lore, over Kevin. The same thoughts loop again and again, so I make my way to the dried pools.

Lore hovers around the skatepark like she was always waiting for me. She wanders into the parking lot alone, balancing on a sleeping on a speed bump.

"Lore." I approach her.

"Yeah?" she asks.

"I think I killed Kevin." I wring my hands together.

She laughs. "Oh, I thought the same thing. For a second, I thought, 'If we'd only had more sex,' or maybe if I was a model girlfriend or a model."

"I think I really did."

"No," she says. "Kevin killed Kevin. Or maybe his parents did. He broke a long time ago. We just stumbled across the pieces and fell in love—at least, I did."

"I'm so sorry."

"I've heard that enough. Sorry, sorry, sorry. Nothing changes." She waves her hands around. "Everyone says, 'Sorry, it will never happen again.' I guess it helps them kill time between suicides."

"But I gave Kevin drugs."

"Who didn't? When we knew each other freshmen year, I'd sneak him all sorts of shit." The wind catches her hair and blows the gray bundle in all directions.

"The coke."

"Okay," she says. "That's what's so weird. The coke. At first, I blamed it for his death. You look for clues, anything that may have changed and brought Kevin to his breaking point. I blamed the coke because I didn't know what else to say."

"Yeah, I gave it to him."

"You gave him something." She pauses. "That's what's weird. They did bloodwork on him. I guess they wanted to bust all his friends for drugs or something. Again, fuck his parents! They found like nothing in his blood. He had a tiny bit of weed. Who doesn't? He had a mega-dose of Prozac. They tested the shit in his coke bag. Some fucking workout powder. You couldn't get Kevin to do a push-up, so I'm not sure what's up with that."

"No coke?"

"None."

I sit down on the speed bump and push my forehead into my hands.

"It sucks that Kevin died," she says. "One day, we'll look at ourselves and say, 'I'm twice the age Kevin was when he died.' By then, his death won't feel that important. Just some long-lost kid. That's what I'm really afraid of. That even I'll look at Kevin's death like the time I broke my wrist in elementary school."

"Calvin would say that your erasers are working well, cutting out the bad shit."

"I don't want it." She steps off the speed bump. "If it doesn't hurt anymore, it'll be like Kevin is gone-gone. Right now, he exists through the pain. If I can feel the hurt, I can feel him. When the hurt disappears, it'll be somehow worse."

There's no real ceremony to how we say goodbye. I just leave her there and she heads somewhere new.

When I get home, I open all the containers on my chest of drawers. I find the creatine container I've been using for the past few weeks. I take a small amount and place it on the table.

When I snort it, I have the most blissful panic attack.

SOMETHING TO MAKE SONGS ABOUT

Go-Karts buzz around the track. Greg and Ken pound the throttle, racing each other in endless circles.

The smell of wet hot dogs hangs in the air. But when the two of them zip past us, a new scent overtakes it. A gasoline smell, like when my dad used to mow the lawn.

I stand behind Sarah, my arm under her shirt so that my forearms press against her warm stomach.

She says, "I don't wanna live here anymore."

"Who does?" I say, not really thinking about it.

"I'm going to Sarah Lawrence next fall, so I won't have to worry. They sent me the admission letter last month. I didn't want to tell you right away. I already knew before visiting." She drums her fingernails against the metal handrail that keeps pedestrians off the track.

Our friends pass by again. Then, they shrink in the distance until they look like *Mario Kart* characters.

"Did you hear me?" Sarah asks.

"Like what? Huh?"

She turns, and my arms drop to my sides. "About getting into Sarah Lawrence. That means I'll live on the East Coast. Like I'm a senior, you know?"

"Well, yeah," I say.

In the dark, her eyes look so dull. "So..." But she doesn't say anything else.

The swell of strained engines fills the gap, then starts to fade.

"Like, so what do you mean?"

"Okay," she says and turns away to face the track. But for some reason, it doesn't feel right to hug her again. "This isn't that easy for me, you know? I know you think it is."

"Like, why don't you want to live here anymore?" I caress a knuckle down her arm, feeling the grit of her sweater against my skin.

She lets the cars pass again, then turns. "Remember *The Jetsons*?"

"Yeah, the cartoon."

"That's the Bay Area," she says. "They have all the fucking gadgets in the damn world. But it's still 'father knows best,' except with search bars. The wives still sit at home. They pick the children up from tutors and team sports. The men sit in glass offices with bean bag chairs. The women go fucking crazy and put every bit of their energy into the kids. The dads don't lift a finger—other than to show disappointment." She faces me again. "You heard what I said?"

"Yeah," I say. "I guess you're right. Like, maybe."

"Look," she says. The Go-Karts pass once again, and her hair blows in the wind. Her eyes don't look dull anymore. They burn.

"Yeah?" I hold eye contact.

"Men never want to grow up," she says. "All this technology helps them master the art of being children forever." She puts her hands on her hips and looks at me.

My body deflates—the opposite of SCAB. But my penis becomes very hard for some reason—at least a B. I want to cover my erection, though. This time, I don't want Sarah to see it. "But why would Sarah Lawrence be different?" I ask.

She looks at me until it hurts to make eye contact with her. "I don't know." She bites her bottom lip. "But it's worth a try."

We watch Greg and Ken get out of their cars and high-five.

She turns away and watches them. Her voice becomes distant: "You know what it means for us, though."

"Yeah."

A song comes on the radio. Something whiny. The sort of song you might want to skate to.

There's nothing to say, so I say, "I hate this song."

The chorus begins and ends.

Sarah speaks, and I almost don't catch what she says.

"I get it, growing up fucking hurts."

Greg and Ken get into Ken's car and disappear, blasting a recording of one of their songs out the window. Greg wrote the song after Jacqueline dumped him. He went to the studio with his guitar and a bag of coke. Everyone thought he looked like a new Greg.

They sing along with the chorus,

"We desire in this broken love."

Their tail lights fade off into the dark.

Orange streetlights cut through the window in bursts, painting Sarah's hair ochre. She keeps her eyes on the road. Even in the tense silence of the drive, I want it to last forever, to never reach our destination, to always look upon Sarah's half-shadowed face. I get the feeling we're racing towards something inevitable and final.

We embrace on the curb in front of my house. She keeps our crotches from touching. A kiss seems out of the equation.

I try to recall the last time I kissed her. I can't remember. I've been taking Klonopin every day, so your guess is as good as mine. It's funny to think that, no matter who you're with, there will always be a last kiss and, most of the time, we won't know when it's just happened.

Sarah passes to the other side of the car and gets in. As she drives away, her backlights bleed into the black much like Greg and Ken's had.

A streetlight hums above me like an annoying insect. I must look like one of the men at the end of an old Hollywood movie. Right before the credits roll.

Now would be a good time to cry. I mean, Humphrey Bogart didn't weep at the end of *Casablanca*, but maybe he should have.

After a couple minutes, it's obvious I'm not going to cry. The combination of Klonopin and Celexa makes that impossible.

Instead, I think how great it'd be if I could play an instrument. Then I could write a song as Greg did. I'd have some sort of trophy from my first big heartache.

Before I head inside, I remember that Sarah sent me countless nude photographs and videos of her masturbating. Between those and the memories, I should have plenty of jerk-off material for the rest of high school.

Looking out my window, the floodlights of an approaching car light up the concrete. The lights make shadows of bushes and trees and then stretch those shadows out long and thin. A sports car comes into view. The engine snorts like a warthog. The car races down the hill and the shadows of bushes snap back to their regular size, like a rubber band at rest. In the quiet neighborhood, no one has a choice but to hear this overwhelming sound. The engine noises fill up everything for a matter of seconds. But then they begin to fade until they're gone.

MOSAIC

There is no narrative, just a mosaic. My life—when I cast its memories upon the darkened walls of my mind, there in a swirl of light, the mangled flesh of my past knits itself together—a mosaic. I reach out to feverish flashes from lost time. I pull forward that day at the carnival. The dusty projector whirs. Memories reopen and, with a need to believe, it appears: that bush of blue raspberries flickering in the dark.

This is what I tell Calvin.

Across from me on the bus, Calvin sits, trying to unravel his sweater into a heap of yarn. He catches a stray thread and tugs.

"I'd give anything to go back and live that day again," I say.

"No, you wouldn't," he says.

"Why?"

The thread snaps, and he tosses it aside. The bus rocks over a pothole. "If I asked you then how you felt, you'd have said you were the most depressed you've ever been," he says, shaking his head. "You only remember the good parts."

"I remember the skin-picking," I say. "Fuck. What I'd give to have skin-picking issues again over the shit now."

He laughs. "Your erasers work so well. Soon, you'll start telling me how sepia-toned the divorce years were."

"That did suck."

"It all sucks." He turns away.

The window frames the passing street.

Calvin leans against the glass, letting the bus shake him about, and he looks tiny.

He looks like he needs a hug, but I'm too scared to give him one.

Here's an image.

Picture Greg.

I find him in the park with Ken. They pace around the grass, soaking their shoes and smoking Camels.

I approach.

"The fuck do you want?" Ken asks me.

"Sorry, dude," I say. "About Jacqueline. Thought you were over it."

Greg looks at me, eyes red. "Who the fuck cares about that whore?"

"Yeah, who cares?" Ken echoes.

"You aren't pissed about it?"

"You don't know shit." Ken shakes his head.

"Yeah, man." Greg sucks hard on his cigarette. He lets the smoke out in a slow hiss through his teeth. "My fucking dad found a load of coke in my room."

"The fuck?" I ask.

"Yeah. Word got around about Kevin. My dad went through my stuff while I was taking a shit. Found it in a drawer." Greg shakes his head. He boots the ground, sending up a clump of mud and grass. "That fucking asshole wants to send me to wilderness."

"Fuck."

"Yeah, fuck," Ken says.

Here's another image.

Picture a woman. You haven't seen her before. She answers the door when I visit Jacqueline's house. Short and with a softer face than even I pictured. Practical, mid-length hair. Dull clothing.

She says her daughter bolted the bedroom door shut.

So, up the stairs again.

Jacqueline lets me in, the lock snapping.

When I step inside, the smell of sweat permeates everything. Jacqueline goes back to her bed. In the background, a Korn song plays—a bass line like a creeping spider.

"I'm sorry," I say.

"About Greg?"

"Yeah."

"Fuck him. I think he fucked that stupid bitch Charlotte, like a bunch of times. You already know that, you were there. I'm not myself."

"Probably," I say.

"I've known it forever. Since before that damn pool party. Maybe that was why I wanted to reconnect with her. I wanted to look her in the eye."

I sit down in her desk chair. Tangles of clothes litter the ground. The comforter hangs off the bed.

Jacqueline settles down and looks at me. "Why'd you come?"

"I don't know. Haven't really, like, talked to you about it yet."

She laughs. "You trying to get seconds or something?"

We sit without talking for a moment.

"Sorry," she says.

"About what?"

"About Sarah." She waves a hand. "I guess we never talked about your breakup much, either."

I shake my head and laugh. "She threw her birthday party yesterday. Age of Aquarius."

"She does that every year." Jacqueline laughs. She puts on a valley girl voice, "Like, my name is Sarah, and I'm like an Aquarius, and I sell drugs because my parents are rich. Also, my dad—you know him— totally like a perv or something. Never pays attention to me."

"I thought you liked her. What about 'Sarah's so cute.' You were full of shit this whole time?"

"She got me Klonopin. Then one day, she just stopped supplying it."

"She... Wait..." I can't explain it, but a wave of panic cuts through the haze. I calculate my odds of having a panic attack, glancing at the exit. Then it's gone again as fast as it came.

"You look so tense," Jacqueline says. "Relax. Fuck. I'd break up with Greg a thousand times if I could get a hold of a single Klonopin. You look like you're gonna have a heart attack if you don't chill."

I shift back and forth on the chair, working the tension out of my abs with my fingers. "How have you felt?"

"Like shit," she says. "Like the worst flu ever or some shit like that. I never feel like I fall all the way asleep anymore."

"That sucks."

She shifts on the bed, propping herself on one elbow to look at me. "My parents started talking about rehab." She rolls her eyes. "The first time I've heard them talk to each other in years. So, if I disappear, you'll know why."

"That would be awful."

"As long as it's in L.A., I'm fine with it." Then she stretches and moans. "The withdrawals come in waves."

"Here." I slide out my wallet and pull a plastic bag from the fold. "I keep this for panic attacks."

She takes the bag. "Klonopin?"

"Yeah."

"You have more?" She rakes her finger through the bag to find the pill.

"No," I say. "It's weeks until my next refill. I guess I've been blowing through them without thinking about it."

She sits up and places the tablet under her tongue. As I watch it disappear into her mouth, I start to sweat, my face gets hot.

Without the pill there just in case, I get a feeling like freefall. I rub my forehead and try to breathe through my nose.

Jacqueline inhales, her face relaxing. "You want a handy or something?" she asks. "You helped me out a lot."

"I would take the offer any other day." I meet her eyes and a jolt of arousal shoots through me. "You know, I've always kinda wanted..."

"I know." She makes eye contact with me.

I shrug. "I think I'm still messed up from the Sarah thing."

"Thanks," she says.

"Why?"

"You coulda said 'yes' to my offer."

The song progresses to a bridge. Jonathan Davis shrieks and screams. I remember the song name, "Chi."

Jacqueline licks her index finger and swizzles it around in the bag. Then she sticks it between her lips and sucks the finger loudly.

"I didn't love Sarah." I look out the window.

She pops the finger out of her mouth. "Figures. No offense, but you and Sarah are like the same person. I don't think you could love someone unless you could control them."

"I don't know."

She shrugs. "It's hard to tell who you actually love." She watches me wring my hands for a moment. "Can you grab the bottle of Seroquel from my dresser?"

"Yeah." I rise from the chair and pull the top drawer open. Inside, several orange pill bottles nestle amongst Jacqueline's underwear.

She says, "You ever ask her about the house?"

"No." I pick up one bottle. It's empty, but I glance at the label.

"Not surprising," she continues. "The place still bothers me."

The bottle once contained Klonopin tablets. The name on the bottle is my own.

"I don't think tech guys understand design."

I don't answer at first. I hold the bottle for a minute, staring at my name. A dizzying feeling mounts inside me. "Yeah," I say, "they don't understand."

"Find the pills?"

My chest deflates. I squeeze the bottle for another moment and put the empty Klonopin bottle back in the drawer. I find the Seroquel and toss it to her.

"Thanks. You look sick," she says.

I sit in the chair again, but I can't face Jacqueline. "It hurt Sarah more than it hurt me."

"No need to be tough about it," Jacqueline says. "Also, I doubt it."

"No." I lean forward. "I think she really loved me."

"It's hard to tell with Sarah," she says. "Must be the Aquarius thing. Want to hear something embarrassing about her?"

I laugh and can face her now. "Sure."

"She saw that bumper sticker, the one that goes, **Not all who wander are lost.** She didn't like it, so she kept trying to rewrite it. This must have been the year before all our dads freaked about Y2K. Sarah sat in class, rewriting that slogan. She wrote, **Some of those who wander really are lost.** She wrote, **Those who wander find themselves.** Shit like that. I bet she goes to Sarah Lawrence and gets it tattooed across her ass."

"Which version will she get?"

"Probably something pretentious like, 'Those who never wander are easiest lost.'"

"Makes sense."

"Thanks for stopping by, at least," she says. "But I gotta sleep."

I leave her.

Outside, the sky hangs heavy, everything lavender and drifting towards violet.

My dad sits in his armchair. He says that he hasn't felt like going to the gym in a while. His co-workers think he's losing his edge. He had a lame date or some shit. Something must be wrong. He drones on and on.

An image comes to me. Kevin, bones snapped, ripped to shreds. The way braces look after a steak dinner. A panicked animal in a barb-wire fence.

The image of Sarah faking death while some sweaty computer nerd ejaculates across her belly.

Then one more image. The way Calvin looked on the bus: deflated.

"I don't have the motivation to do anything anymore," my dad says.

I pause, thinking for a second, not really listening to him. I say, "I think you should double your creatine dose."

Every hero's journey has lied to you. There is no narrative.

Life is a mosaic of suffering. It stretches on and on like an endless film reel. All I've done is clip a few segments for you to witness.

Every memory becomes a golden age beside the present horror.

Let's return to the image of Calvin by the bus window. Keep it in your mind.

Behind him, houses flicker by—a zoetrope of the city. A split second from every life, moving in a constant cascade.

Picture a young man. He will never be the tallest or the shortest person in the room. His head leans against the window. We hiss to a stop, and he stands, dragging his backpack to his shoulders. We exit the bus together.

He says, "Remember that night we walked to the top of the hill overlooking our houses."

We stand at the corner. Our street stretches before us. If one squints down it, then, like a cascade, memories materialize. I gaze through my past. In relief, that same hill rises in the distance. I return and tell him that I remember that night.

He says, "I told you that I dreamed my feet were full of bees, that when I looked at the city, all I saw were honeycombs. A thousand repeating patterns. The bees don't know they're building honeycombs. They build until they die. Even if everything around them crumbles to nothing, they'll keep trying to build those honeycombs. The city below—a thousand golden clusters. Then I thought about myself. That, inside me, if I cut myself open, I might see a thousand similar clusters. That the world and its repeating determinism crept into my own insides, running in my blood. That's when I wanted to scream and scream."

I scratch the back of my neck, and it feels hot to the touch. "We just have to protect ourselves from feeling like that."

He says, "Last night, I was reading and came across a new word: misericord." He looks up to that hill we once climbed. "The word refers to a dagger that knights carried with them. A blade thin enough to slip between gaps in plate armor. When a knight lay dying on the battlefield, a foe or a friend—it wouldn't matter at that point—would deliver a mercy blow. Yes, they stood strong but always planned for the moment their armor would fail them."

I don't know what to say, so I tense my chest and rub my palms against my pecs to check my progress.

How about something else?

At school, my chest locks up in class. Inflating my lungs feels like breathing through a straw from a pig's stifling guts. I dig in my wallet for the last Klonopin, then remember that I gave it to Jacqueline. My teacher sends me out in front of everyone. None of my friends are in the class, so there's that, at least.

When I reach the office, I want to fall on the cement. A nurse with a smooth, dark tan checks on the color of my fingernails.

"You're getting enough oxygen," she says. "Look how pink your nails are."

"Help me," I say.

She turns and shuffles around on a desk. She must be searching for the right medicine. Maybe she has a stash of Klonopin in a drawer.

Instead, the nurse hands me a folded-up copy of a local newspaper. "Here," she says. "Read something boring; it'll help."

Then she leaves me alone.

When I unfold the paper, the first article catches my attention. Beside it—a photo of a familiar house—a house with a pool house out back.

But here's the story.

A Silicon Valley venture capitalist bought a house. This was back before the whole Enron thing. He said no one touched the listing. It sat on the market for close to a year. He'd had a windfall and wanted to move his family closer to downtown.

The article's author jumped aside for a minute. Said that Menlo Park was a home for businessmen; that the city boasted the longest-running train station in California; that this VC followed in the footsteps of countless men before him: all local paper shit.

So, the VC, he asked around. Why did the house sit on the market that long? He went with some buddies to The Oasis. They split pitchers and got to talking. He said they filled him in, and it all clicked.

It clicks for me when the article details the names of all the previous owners. Stories we've all heard.

The man who sliced his date up. Paramedics found her lying on the parquet floors. He tried to flee the Bay Area, but they caught him trapped in traffic.

The coach who'd retired in his forties from business and assaulted a whole team of high school girls.

The coder who kept a woman locked in one of the upstairs bedrooms for a month—Sarah's bedroom.

They each left a wound on the home, and each owner tore down a piece of it and constructed some new extension. Dull, violent men— and Sarah's words come back to me—just the same men there's always been but with gadgets and search bars.

At the end of that line, Sarah's father bought the home.

"The first thing I did was rip out the downstairs family room. I installed a personal office. The business landscape has changed since the '80s..."

I set down the newspaper. No one sees me leave the office and walk home.

At home, I sit on my bed and look through some pictures Sarah posted to MySpace.

Photos in her living room, all her friends posing. A banner above their heads reads, **The Age of Aquarius**. Bell-bottom jeans flare out around ankles and floral prints bloom. The guys half-button their silk tops, showing their chests. A man with a peace medallion necklace and a polished belt buckle sits next to Sarah in one of the pictures. His arm hangs over her shoulder. She smiles, displaying the two-finger peace sign, the flash coloring Sarah's eyes red, which reminds me of a white bunny. Her hair—woven with flowers—flows down her shoulders. Then, I see them in the background, red cups in hand: Floyd and Brennon.

I zoom in on the photo, cropping them out, leaving just Sarah in frame. I look at the photograph for several minutes. I touch the laptop, my finger indenting the soft screen. My finger presses against Sarah's chin. I run my finger up her cheek and down to her chin again. I zoom in on the picture so that her head stretches to actual size. The picture pixilates and distorts. I run my finger up to her cheek again. I place four fingers against the screen and pretend I'm running my fingers through her hair. I lean to the screen as if to smell the flowers sewn into her hair. I kiss the screen. I try to remember what her Dior lip gloss tasted like or the flavor of her Chanel. I look at the picture and see if I can figure out which one it is. The zoom distortion breaks her lips into overlapping squares. White squares where the light hits them over the reddish-mauve skin.

I can't tell what gloss she's wearing.

I close my eyes and put myself in the room. There must be music playing. Maybe No Doubt. If the energy hits the roof, it's something like "Hey Baby." If everyone wants to mellow out, maybe it's "Don't Speak." In each photograph, a different song, or a different part of a song would have been playing. I try to put things together.

I see Sarah in front of me. She laughs at a joke. I walk up to her. She turns and smiles at me. I take her hand. I run my hand through her hair. But when I do this, the reverie vanishes. I'm back in my room in front of the laptop. I'm trying to remember what her hair texture felt like. I realize I didn't run my hands through her hair enough times.

That's when I get up and walk the many blocks to the skatepark. The thousand dollhouses tower over me.

The skatepark at night makes one imagine the apocalypse after the apocalypse, when even the survivors can't take it anymore.

I find a way into the bathroom, prying at a window and slipping up and over the sill on my stomach. In the beam of a flashlight, I fish in the dark for Calvin's message—the one he wrote after Kevin's death.

In the tense silence of this narrow chamber, I read.

When I first learned the piano, I sat in the back of the orchestra, right beside the double bass.

That's where I met Kevin. But that's also where a thought occurred to me. We played dozens of songs and performed before auditoriums of parents and friends. Each time I pressed my hands into the keys, I brought something to life. Something beautiful. The notes sung through the air, and there they were, freed from the piano, from my hands and body, vibrant and, above all, existing. A momentary beauty. We strained our ears as they rang out, searching for their last whispers.

This was back when Kevin existed. Now he only exists in memories.

Oh, memories.

Memories are mayflies.

I spoke to a school counselor who told me that. That memories couldn't hurt me because they no longer existed. That was, of course, after I told her about my memories. Even now, you'll get no satisfaction in uncovering my past. I was hurt in a way that never leaves you, and may those memories fade with me.

Memories are a plea spoken in a dead tongue.

So, I took it upon myself to rid my mind of these memories. The more I tried to destroy them, the more I felt like I was destroying myself. But I was standing beside you, and I passed among you, and you could see me and hear my voice and look me in the eyes, but you would never know what I fought inside.

Memories are shadows, bleached away by the sun.

While I write this, we mourn another loss. He fades from our memories, those formless things, so much like the notes I once pulled from the piano. Even this day is nothing but potential energy. Perhaps that's why I placed these words where you can scrub them away, to surrender to that fact.

The way we trot out our memories is the most deluded form of transient art.

I can see why people want to believe in ghosts.

We're almost done here. But I have a little more to tell.

Last Call

Rush hour traffic snakes up and down Santa Cruz Avenue. It twists around the corners that spill onto Alameda de las Pulgas and Sand Hill Road. A backed-up snake with scales the angry color of brake lights. In the opposite direction, another snake moves. One beast squeezes through avenues toward 101; the other snake runs towards 280. You may add a decorative "the" to the highway names if you please.

Picture this the way a crow might. This pair: a great squirming caduceus. Watch it slither between mansions. Listen to its incessant blaring.

I receive the call. A little buzzing in my jeans pocket.

"Hey, dude," I say.

An inhalation of breath travels from the speaker.

"Calvin?" I press the speaker hard to my ear, trying to line up the little mesh speaker holes with my ear hole.

"Dude," he says. In the background, the evening traffic drones.

"Where are you?"

"I *can't* sleep," he says.

"Yeah, dude," I say. "You've told me that."

"I can't *can't* sleep," he says.

"What do you mean?"

"I'm sorry."

"Tell me where you are."

He sighs.

"Like you're starting to sound scary, dude." I step out into my backyard, traveling towards the fence like it'll give me a better signal.

"Some people can live with things for—" He stops like the signal broke up, but the sound of traffic never breaks.

I reach the fence and crane my neck towards Calvin's place. A dark room through his window. The glass reflects the sour day.

"I'm just sorry," he says. "That's all."

"Come on," I say. "I'll come, like, hang out with you for a bit. Jacqueline can drive me over."

"It won't matter."

"What do you mean?"

Silence lasts long enough for my stupid brain to start putting things together.

"Hey," I say.

"Yeah?"

"You down by the used book store? Across from the tracks?"

"Just left a few minutes ago," he says.

"Don't go," I say. "Let me get Jacqueline. We'll be right over."

"Yeah."

"Don't go."

Then the call drops.

My shins ache when I get to Jacqueline's house. I pound on the front door. The knocks bring Jacqueline's dog. The sound of nails scratching wood. A muted sort of crying.

I shout Jacqueline's name then pound again with the butt of my fists. The dog runs away from the door, little skitters disappearing.

Jacqueline answers the door with a down comforter wrapped around her shoulders. "What the fuck?" Her voice lacks any volume.

"You didn't answer your phone," I say.

"So what?"

"I'm worried about Calvin."

"I'm worried about myself." The skin under her eyes looks dry and scaly.

"He's down at the tracks. We gotta go to him."

"Why?" She shivers and tightens the blanket over her chest, covering the pajama shirt beneath it.

"I'm worried about him. He didn't sound good."

"I've been gone for a week," she says. "Sitting here, shivering and feeling like death. All you gave me was one fucking pill."

"I'm sorry." I gesture as if to get her moving. "Can we drive there? We have to hurry."

"Fuck that. You have to be kidding."

"Come on. Please."

"If we go..." she says and pauses.

"What?"

"If we go, I'm not getting out of the car, okay?"

"Yeah, that's fine."

"Give me a few minutes."

Take out your phone.
Call your best friend.
Repeat as needed.

When Jacqueline drags herself from the house, I get a robotic message telling me I've filled up Calvin's voicemail box.

Inside Jaqueline's car, she twists the climate control until we see red. She reverses out into the street. The back tires trundle over the steep curb and the loose suspension shakes us up.

The Lexus butts up against the snake when Jacqueline's tries for a main road. We backpedal. Then we loop around, sliding into a side street, and weaving past an old cemetery.

"Hurry."

We merge into a series of avenues. Wide streets stretch for blocks between us and El Camino Real: the last great hurdle. My foot keeps a rabid sort of time with whatever album Jacqueline keeps in the disc changer.

"You gotta stomp it."

Jacqueline dips into the accelerator. Her body wobbles with the suspension. A boxer in the final round.

The Lexus eats away at the blacktop ahead of us. For a moment, we aren't a car. The road isn't passing beneath us. Instead, we ride the serpent as it swallows everything in our path. We nestle between the eyes of the ouroboros. That's when the ending meets the beginning, because we never see it coming. No matter how many fucking times this sort of thing happens, we never see it.

The right front tire goes from grating pavement to an open freefall.

It strikes the bottom of the pothole and the hole's mouth tears the rubber open. The burst resounds like a cannonade and a hiss follows.

Then the dragging, squealing sound of the wheel.

The car fishtails and swipes across the road with big, drunken strokes.

My head strikes the glass of my window.

Jacqueline grips the wheel, yanked from her stupor.

With spinning and screaming, the protesting car comes to rest along the side of the road.

We get out of the car before either of us says a word.

The dead tire weeps in the gutter.

We both stand on the sidewalk. My head aches; my pulse beats in the sore spot. We stand in front of someone's yard. A flower bed grows up to the sidewalk. A little retaining wall rises behind the bed, and early spring flowers—still in their infancy—dangle over the precipice.

"You should have paid more attention," I say.

"My mom's gonna be so fucking mad." She looks at the wheel.

"The fuck is wrong with you?" My voice sounds dry and jagged. "You. What the fuck?"

She turns to me. "I wouldn't have even driven the car. You wanted to go so fucking bad, just begging me and whining and pissing me off."

"You don't get to be pissed off," I say. "You have no fucking idea."

"It's not my fault." She swipes her arm up and down. "We're in this position because you couldn't stop being you. You had to nag and obsess, nag and obsess. Fuck you."

A sports car whips by behind me. The engine growls so loud that it raises my hackles.

I grind my molars together. "We can't get to Calvin," I say. "It's like forever still."

"Then run there," she says. "I'm done."

"You can't quit now."

"Well, I do. This shit didn't work."

"What do you mean?"

"I said what I mean." She crosses her arms. "It was a nice try. But it's over. I have to call my mom or something and get her to call a tow truck or some shit like that. I don't know."

"Drive on the rim or something," I say.

"No," she says. "I told you that I gave it a try. Too late now."

I turn away and suck in air hard. I pace, pull out my phone, and hit a full mailbox. Then I see a decorated mailbox in front of me, a little light illuminates the street number.

I punch it, which hurts my fist and doesn't even dent the box. "Fuck."

"Calm the fuck down." She lets out a deep breath.

I suck and suck on air, and my head turns to static, and I suck once more after that. My chest burns and, no matter how much air I inhale, it doesn't feel like enough. My lungs still feel like popped balloons or popped tires.

"I'm serious," Jacqueline says. "All that fucking anger isn't good for you. You walk around with your shoulders in your fucking ears. I knew you'd snap for like forever."

I rub and pull on my face again and again like I'm trying to remove a latex mask. "You have no fucking idea." My voice sounds far away. My ears feel congested. A piercing ringing begins. "That's my best friend. You don't do that. You don't let them go like that."

"He's fine, I think," she says. "Since when did any of us have best friends anymore?"

"Fuck you."

"No wonder Sarah dumped you if this is how you talk to women."

"Sarah only cares about herself."

"Sarah wanted someone who could calm the fuck down once in a while. Who didn't obsess over everything. Someone who was good in bed."

"I can't believe you."

She puts her hands on her hips and shakes her head. "Pathetic." That's when I boil over.

She bites her bottom lip and we're grabbing at each other, fingers digging into shoulders, and feet shuffling. She hits one of my ears with the heel of her palm. We grapple, and I shove her away with both hands. She sits down hard, crushing some of the blooming flowers. Her eyes widen. She looks up at me. Her staring, dazed eyes start to water.

She shakes her head and cries and snot runs down her face. She tilts her head back until it rests against the small retaining wall. "So that's what was in there the whole time," she says. "I thought maybe you'd be different."

I back up and bump into the car. A cold sheet travels through my body. I lean there and try to slow my breathing. My body deflates, and I feel so small, shrinking. Above us, the skies threaten rain. I swear I smell something like ozone.

Our gazes meet once more. Something hangs in the air between us. The sidewalk stretches like a flat gray ocean.

From: Jaqueline De Leon <penguin_grrl89@hotmail.com>
   To: <no_shoes@hotmail.com>
   Date: 02/28/2006 7:46PM

   Subject: Jacarandas

   Hey,

   it's me JAQUELINE. everyone is starting to get ready for bed but since i have been really good at everything they let me write some emails. i don't know if i forgive you or not yet. when i get out of here i might have to punch you in the nose so that we will be even. maybe when you're not expecting it. though i hope we can talk and that you'll apologize again and that we can still be friends.

i know how tough things have been (haven't things been tough for all of us?) maybe ill make you cut your little finger off like this one movie about Japanese gangsters my dad made me watch. but what i really hope is that youll love me but not like in a boyfriend/girlfriend way but in a way where you'd never think of shoving me. i know at least there is more to each of us than our worst qualities (they taught me that here) i think sometimes that we can only see each other the way we see a city from the window of a plane. its hard to figure out what details to focus on. sometimes i try to take the whole city in at once. sometimes i just count the number of pools in backyards.

anyway i'll tell you a little bit about what i've been up to. they drove me down here a few days after i last saw you. it felt weird driving all the way to sunny L.A. and then going right into a big building with cold AC and tinted windows like a casino.

the first day was great because they let me sit on this couch in a waiting room. everything smelled the way a doctor's office smells. that sour smell you know? someone must clean it all the time.

a guy in a polo shirt came in and he sat across from me and put a hand out. he said that EVERYTHING WILL BE ALL RIGHT and i cried like a little kid. when people say stuff like that it makes you go weak in the knees. try it sometime. say EVERYTHING WILL BE ALL RIGHT to someone and watch the way they get all wobbly.

but then they started asking me all these questions. they had me fill out papers. felt like i was back in school. they still do this every day. they check things like my weight, my blood pressure, heart rate, how much food i'm eating, the hours i sleep each night. sometimes a nurse in donald duck scrubs comes to suck blood out of my arm and then that's a lot more numbers to look at. it's like i'm invisible to them or something until they can draw me up out of a lot of numbers and categories. like when they've completed all these forms then JACQUELINE can exist. they break you down to a million parts. from your hair to your guts. they used to do this thing with animals, pull their guts out and "read their guts" to predict what was going to happen. they're reading all of our guts and not just in rehab. all the time.

there are a lot of other girls here and a lot of them remind me of me. they let us have caffeine and in the other building i see the girls that are 18 get cigarettes and sometimes i can sneak a smoke from one of them. this older girl said to me that they get you clean by hooking you on the two most addicting drugs which are caffeine and nicotine. she also showed me this good song that i think youd like called LIME TREE ARBOUR and i listen to it when i sit by the pool and pretend that everything is normal. The song is either about love and feeling safe or its about dying and pain and i cant think about life in general.

one of the girls gets no doze pills sometimes and she beats them to dust with the bottom of a water glass or a snapple bottle and then she snorts them up in lines. we did that once remember? another girl takes a lot of benadryl and spaces out. they give me medicine but they measure it just right. Wellbutrin and Celexa in little paper cups. then each day they ask me what my mood is like.

what does a 3 on the suicide scale even mean?

some days i talk with a big group of girls like me. we sit around and dig through our memories. it's neat. time feels like it paused when i got here, so we just go through our day and live in our memories at group.

some other days i go and talk with a woman in a room alone. you know what it makes me think of? remember back a few years ago? this was back when i still slept with so many stuffed animals on my bed that i could barely turn left or right (group made me remember this) i used to keep the stuffed animals until the seams across their bellies split and they bled stuffing on my bed.

I used to write notes on a sheet of torn up notebook paper. wrote really small. i would write things like *i hate my dad so much. sometimes i want to take a knife and stab him in the face while he's sleeping because he hurt my mom and she wont show me the hurt. i don't trust him. my mom ignores me. i swear it's only a matter of time before my dad tries to touch me and my mom won't do anything because we have money and live in a big house and things like that don't exist in a world of big houses and lambos and private schools.*

i took all those notes and folded them up so small and stuck them into the stuffed animal bellies. it made me feel a little better. taking all that hate i felt and sticking it inside of a stuffed beagle that my grandma gave me once. the one with the sad eyes (the beagle not my grandma)

but i didn't want to talk about stuffed animals. i wanted to talk about the year i still had stuffed animals. one day someone from the office called my third period class. we're all silent doing our work and the teacher hangs the phone up and tells me in front of the whole class that the office wants to see me. i don't know why.

that walk down the hall to the office gave me cramps. my stomach felt all hot and awful. then i got there and no one had died, i wasn't in trouble. they just wanted me to see a school counselor. so they led me into her little office. i remember how she looked. way younger than my mom. super pretty. beautiful curly hair. she sat me down in a chair and between her and me sat her desk with a box of tissues in the middle. it looked like it was always placed there like salt and pepper shakers at a restaurant.

she tells me that she brought me into the office because she heard that i might need to talk to someone about how i felt. the first thing i thought was *who said something about me?* but i didn't. instead i just nodded. she told me that the office was a place where i could say anything i wanted to. that no one else would know what we talked about (which i didn't believe).

we sat there in silence together a few minutes. then i told her that i thought i was doing okay. that i didn't feel that bad. she told me that feeling bad was okay and that she just wanted to help. the funny thing is this. inside my head i had a thousand things i wanted to say to her. my mind felt like angry bees stinging the inside of my skull and wanting to be let out.

she told me that i could tell her anything. anything at all.

the backs of my eyes felt hot and itchy and the back of my head sweated and i thought that if i could just tell her exactly how i felt that it may feel so good.

but i couldn't and i talked to her a little bit about life and then the bell rang and i needed to go get my binder.

have you ever felt that way? like you just wish you could tell someone how you felt without having to say anything? that the feelings inside are so hard to describe. you wish you could jump over description and get right to the heart of them.

remember that concert we went to on my birthday back in October? they played that song i love called NAKED AS WE CAME. you didn't see it or anything but i cried in the dark and flickering lights of that autumn night. because sometimes a song is a song and it's fun but sometimes it's more than that. inside our skulls everything is dark, just our brain and our self alone in the black. but that right song or phrase will bridge that gap and it's like someone cracked open my head and cracked open their head and we saw each other. maybe naked is the right word or maybe it isn't.

in that office with that counselor I wanted to scream **PLEASE JUST SPLIT OPEN MY SKULL SO YOU CAN SEE ME.**

at the end of the year she called me in again. that day was hot and felt like summer coming. she asked me how i was feeling and if i was still feeling sad and mad even though i never really told her that i was feeling sad and mad.

i said it didn't matter because we were about to graduate and in high school it would be better.

once again we just sat in silence and the bell rang after a while.

i said **SORRY** and left her sitting there looking sadder than i felt. maybe it wasn't just her that understood me but also me that understood her, and **THAT** really scared me. i could feel how she felt without her saying a word. maybe that's why i told everyone i wanted to be a shrink. they say "shrink" still, but really they should compare it to trepanning instead.

but after that second meeting i went home and sat on my bed and looked at my room. all of a sudden i wanted to hide all my stuffed animals so i did. i boxed them up and sealed them and put them in the garage.

no one really noticed.

now i'm here and they ask me the same sorts of questions and it's like nothing has changed since middle school and i don't even have stuffed animals. what did fugazi say about being **SO TIRED?** are sheep counting me yet? that's exactly how i feel. there is another example. that song pierced into my head.

i wonder what greg is doing. he doesn't get emails where he is and that might be good for him. i bet he's hiking around in the woods and painting mud across his face and playing like he's rambo. you know guys. they always have to make their pain seem heroic and special. they tell themselves the same sorts of stories over and over about being heroes and becoming more powerful. he probably thinks all that fresh air makes him freer. but while he hikes through the forests or the deserts they are typing his weight and blood pressure and happiness scores in a computer somewhere. he will come back and tell great stories about wilderness camp and call himself a recovering addict and try to use it to pick up girls. now we have myspace where we can record our thoughts and the songs we like and the number of days we've been sober.

a quick aside. the problem with guys is this. girls will say things about hating their bodies or harming themselves or thinking about suicide or falling to pieces and you guys look at us like we can't feel real pain. you look at our bodies and think no one could feel that way about ourselves while looking the way we look. you think all our pain and sorrow is trivial. that might hurt more than anything. that's also why i forgave charlotte. it must be awful being overlooked the way she is. like she's just a prop or an unimportant character. it must make her feel like she's shrinking. maybe that's why she starves herself. then she can see actual shrinking and not just feel it, if you know what i mean.

i know i rambled a lot. i sort of skipped over the thing that probably matters the most to you. that's calvin. you know, don't worry about calvin. i'm sure he's fine. maybe his parents sent him to wilderness too and he just didn't tell you. i bet he will be back soon. his birthday is next week right? i bet he shows up for that at least. remember how we used to go to class with a bushel of balloons tied to our backpack straps on our birthdays like we were trying to fly away from middle school? anyway. i bet calvin comes back soon. try checking his house again. maybe he got a vacation. i know how you worry yourself sick over others. it's the best thing about you and the most hateful thing.

before i left i read this great book by EVE BABITZ. she talked about the jacaranda trees in L.A. how they bloom each year and how when they bloom it's a sort of magical special time. what's cool is that when the jacarandas start blooming that's when they'll let me out of here. i bet i'll have a lot of days sober. well sober from everything except caffeine and nicotine.

maybe i can meet you in the bay and after i punch you in the nose we can go into my garage with a box cutter and read the guts of all my old stuffed animals.

write me back
your friend

JAQUELINE

:-P

ON DARK NIGHTS WHEN THE FULL MOON IS IN CANCER

You have options when searching someone out.

You can stop wringing your hands and, instead, ring doorbells and landlines and cellphones, too. Rattle the door with the blunt of your fist. Use the sharp of your knuckles on windowpanes.

Without an answer, you can settle at a spot in the street and ambush anyone rolling in and out of the garage.

But maybe they slip by.

Also, no one is truly an island. Work the spiderweb. Find friends, family, friends-of-the-family, doctors, pharmacists, and vague acquaintances. You'll draw a lead. That, or you'll get the sense they're all conspiring to keep something from you.

Look for lights in windows. Count days like running down a potential vacation.

The network we live in leaves paper trails. Sniff out news articles. Comb obituaries, school papers, newsletters, and police blotters.

Drag the waters. The conspiracy has to break. Someone will tell you the truth.

After a few nights, a car slips into his driveway as soft as a brushstroke. You tumble out of the house, forgetting your shoes, the grit of asphalt digging into your heels—

The door closes before you can catch sight. Is that a light in a hallway window? You clamor to the door and raise your fist. But you can't...

Behind the door, your answers are waiting. You haven't seen him in class for weeks. What is even happening?

Maybe closure would mean pain and acceptance, but you can't knock on the door. You can't knock because maybe waiting is torture, but torture produces a bit of hope. You want to just see him again, walking down the street or standing in the springtime sunshine. But this can't be how you find your answer. So, you walk away, feet puckering on the pebbled walkway. A song ending in a diminished chord.

Picture a field. A walnut tree grasps for the sun at the edge of the schoolyard. Its roots knuckle their way out of the soil. A spot in the schoolyard away from the clamor of the blacktop and busy lunch tables.

Picture a boy. He will never be the tallest or the shortest person in the room. He keeps his hair the way a surfer would. He stood beneath the walnut tree on some long-ago weekday, one dirty New Balance upon a lump of roots. A hand in the pocket of his denim shorts. He wore a T-shirt and...

But now you're not so sure what the T-shirt said. This lost detail cooks the skin on the back of your neck. Grasping in the dark, trying to determine if it was Target or Old Navy. Maybe it was gray with parallel stripes. Maybe a solid neutral color. If you can't remember that image and, if that was such an important image and time still swallowed it up, then one day time will swallow up the rest of your memories about the young man, the one you can't seem to find, and without new memories of him, how will you be able to think about him at all?

Across the street, a small group of guys walk. They laugh too loud. Name badges hang from their belt loops. Button-up shirts and briefcases. They drive Mercedes cars and BMW luxury sedans.

You look back at the spot at the tree, expecting to cry. Cry because the boy isn't there anymore. This isn't the day you watched him prop his foot on a gnarl of roots. The boy isn't there because this isn't then, and he isn't there now because you haven't found him anywhere. But knowing this doesn't tug tears out of your eyes. Nothing pierces the medicinal haze. If the wind blows a while longer and irritates your eyes so bad that they drop a tear, then at least you'll have something to show for your effort.

The men laugh again, and it feels like taking a bite out of a white-hot lightbulb. You could be doing something more productive than looking at a tree. Maybe studying for Stanford. Maybe beating people to death with a copy of *The Mask of Sanity* until someone wails, "Please, won't someone stop that man?"

Pick a few of your favorite songs. You could listen to Andre Nickatina and Equipto reflecting on their lives in "Caught in a Verse." That's the sort of song that will make you cry.

Every time you go to reflect though, the fog banks roll in, and everything around you becomes gray and silent. Some people might find this calming, but as the fog cuts off the rest of the world you think that some days you'd rather be screaming and raving and breaking down if it meant you'd get through this. You could also pick something like that new Korn single about how no one understands you but music always will.

So, trust in music.

Look at that tree and sing and scream. If a couple of guys can crow over mergers and acquisitions, then you can howl yourself hoarse.

Now check in on those tears.

Still nothing, I guess.

So, amp it up.

Think about the last child you saw losing it in the detergent aisle. Picture the way their arms swung in frantic windmills. They stomped and sneered and scraped their tonsils raw.

Do your best impersonation; hope for tears; repeat as needed.

Back at the blacktop, floodlights switch on. They cast the scene in orange.

Blocky tables hulk in the artificial light. Tomorrow, kids will eat lunch there. They will never know that you went to your former grade school, on the birthday of your best friend, and pictured the way he looked long ago.

Tomorrow's children will never know the tantrum you threw. They'll never see the twisting face. The way you screamed and shouted, but never cried. Instead, they will eat bad-smelling cafeteria food. Custodians and seagulls will clean up after them.

In the parking lot where teachers and staff park their mid-sized sedans, you turn and glance back.

Everything looks so small. The classroom doors. The basketball hoops, four square courts, and wall-ball walls.

Tables for mice and a playground for squirrels.

Here's what you do.

Go home and walk into your backyard. From a spot along the fence, you can crane your neck and peer into the backyards of adjacent houses.

With your chest to the fence and your head cranked to the side, you can spot a second-story window. The room beyond the pane remains dark.

Press into the fence as hard as you can for a better angle. You should feel the thuds of your heart against the fencepost. Use your ears and listen for signs of life between the beats.

You look—still dark.

You hear—nothing.

But I'll whisper you a secret.

If you repeat this process every night then, on some nights—if you stare long enough—you may catch a glimpse of...

There he is!

Just for a moment, maybe a figure. What appears like a young man who gazes out the window.

He surveys the hills that form a wall between him and the Pacific Ocean. The hills where fog crests overtop like a great wave.

Keep looking—I know you'll find him.

Thanks for reading! Find more transgressive fiction (poems, novels, anthologies) at: Outcast-Press.com

TikTok, X & Instagram: @OutcastPress

Facebook.com/OutcastPress1

Amazon, Kindle, Target, Barnes & Nobel

Email proof of your review to OutcastPress@gmail.com & we'll mail you a free bookmark/sticker!

From the greasy spoon to gourmet sit-in, these 20 stories curated by Craig Clevenger (author of *The Contortionist's Handbook, Mother Howl,* and *In Filth It Shall Be Found*) show diners are where heists are plotted, bodies get dumped, and police are tipped off. They host drug deals to premeditated murder and mob mutiny. It's all fluorescent-lit, fly-riddled entertainment to the drunk, recovering, or wish-they-were.

MORE FROM OUTCAST PRESS

How would you feel if today was your last day on Earth? Lotus is the part of yourself you're afraid and ashamed by, all the bad thoughts you shove inside the darkest corner of your brain. This 18-poem literary/visual arts collection explores death, sex, drugs, drinking, honesty, and the after-life.

With rock 'n' roll flare and an appreciation for nature, Austin Davis unravels everything from teenage degeneracy to the cosmos in under 50 pages.

ABOUT THE AUTHOR

Twitter: **@Remo_PM**

Instagram: **@Remo_Nassutti_Writer**

Remo Nassutti is a fiction writer and editor from the San Francisco Bay Area. His short works appear via *34 Orchard, Heads Dance Press, 3-B Publishing,* and *Shoot Your Eye Out.* He holds a bachelor's in sociology from CSU Chico and a master's in sociology from Colorado State University. He resides in Southern California with his wife, Brittan, and is working on two new novels: an ode to music and Los Angeles, as well as a follow-up to *Blue Raspberry.*

You can also find him on Substack posting horror analysis, short stories about rock stars, and some reprints of aforementioned magazine fiction.

www.SubStack.com/@RemoNassutti